The THIRD
Passenger

Also by Caroline Crane

The THIRD Passenger

Caroline Crane

DODD, MEAD & COMPANY
NEW YORK

1   2   3   4   5   6   7   8   9   10

Library of Congress Cataloging in Publication Data

Crane, Caroline.
    The third passenger.

    I. Title.
PS3553.R2695T5   1983   813'.54   82-19923
ISBN 0-396-08132-0

For James and Laurel

1

Tuesday, like the two days preceding it, had been rainy and heavy with fog. At three o'clock the rain stopped. The afternoon was damp, misty, and unseasonably mild. Ellen Hastings Corder took advantage of the break in the weather to drive into Holland Mills and finish her Thanksgiving shopping. It was better than waiting until the next day when the store would be crowded, and it gave the children a badly needed outing.

Badly needed. She thought she would go crazy in the supermarket with a three-year-old and a four-year-old who had been cooped up for two days.

"Take it easy till we get home," she told them. "Then you can play outside for a while." They whooped with joy. She only hoped it wouldn't start to rain again.

Her luck held, but it was getting dark by the time she pulled into her driveway.

"Stay out of the puddles," she warned the children as they scrambled from the car. She did not expect them to hear her or pay attention, and they didn't. If they had been bigger, they could have helped her carry in the groceries. Six heavy bags, including a frozen twenty-two-pound turkey. She was hosting Thanksgiving dinner for her parents in the new house she and Mike had bought last April.

She left the groceries on the kitchen counter and went

out again to put away the car. Mike always told her to back it into the garage. It was easier to get it out the next time, he said. She couldn't see what difference it made whether it was easier to get the car in or out; it all added up to the same thing.

She turned on the headlights. They caught Natalie across the lawn, inspecting the withered flower garden. With a four-year-old's persistence, Natti had asked her over and over again throughout the fall why flowers had to die.

Backward and forward she drove, awkwardly turning the car in a space that was too small. It was all right to run up onto the grass a little bit, but not to hit the bushes.

And then the hard part. She never could figure out whether it worked better to look over her shoulder or into the mirror. She should have turned on the garage light. This was the worst time of day, when the half-light and shadows made everything hard to see.

She eased the car backward. She felt it hit something. Felt it, but didn't hear it. She fumbled for the brake.

A bush, she thought, opening her door. The car lurched. She gasped and slammed at the brake again. She hadn't put it in park, my God! She had left it in reverse and forgotten the parking brake.

She sat for a moment, calming her heart. Mom had always worried about her heart, even though there was nothing really wrong with it. Mom always worried about her and never about Diane. It was as if they trusted Diane to be strong and to survive.

A bush. It really must have been the forsythia, although she thought it would have made a scratchy sound, but maybe she didn't hit it hard enough for that. She swung her legs out of the car and walked back. And when she saw what was there, she began to scream.

2

The call came late in the evening. Diane Hastings had worked a twelve-hour day and had come home reluctantly to the New York apartment that was lonely without her little son. She was on her way to bed when the telephone rang.

"Diane? Dear?"

She felt a prickle of alarm. It was her mother, who lived in Holland Mills. Who always retired early and never made phone calls after nine.

"What's up, Mom?"

The word *Mom* was inadvertent. For years she had not called her parents anything but "you."

Her mother took no notice. "I'm sorry, dear. I think you'd better come home. Something's happened to Kevin."

"*Kevin?*" What had they done to Kevin?

Wasn't it enough what they had done to her?

"It's quite serious," her mother said. "I think you'd better come."

"How serious? What happened?"

He's dead, she thought. He's dead. What am I going to do?

"He's in a— He's unconscious, dear." The voice sounded watery, near tears. "He had some bleeding. Inside. They gave him a blood transfusion, but it turns out he has a very rare type and the hospital blood bank is—"

"What type? Does he have AB negative?"

"Something like that. Yes, that's what it is."

"But I have it! I'm AB negative. I could have given him blood. Why didn't you call me? Why?"

"I've been trying to get you all evening," her mother said plaintively. "I didn't know about the blood, but I did try to call you. I'm home now. Dad and Ellen are still at the hospital."

"How bad is it? Tell me. What happened? I want to know."

"He was in the driveway. A car went in to turn around. They didn't—they just didn't see him. Ellen didn't know till they drove away and she saw him lying there."

Hit by a car. She thought she was going to be sick. Had he actually been run over?

Her legs weakened under her, and she slid from the sofa arm down into the cushions. This couldn't be real. It was some sort of nightmare to show her what could happen, but it hadn't really.

"When? When was it?"

"This afternoon," said her mother. "Late in the afternoon. I kept trying to call you, but—"

"I was at the office. Did you try calling the office?"

"We—wanted to know how he was before—"

"You didn't know how to tell me, right?"

Because it was Ellen. Ellen's carelessness. He was only three years old. Too young to be left alone outside, but Ellen didn't care.

"Darling, we wanted to know how he was so we wouldn't upset you more than necessary."

"You hoped they'd send him home with a Band-Aid and I'd never find out, didn't you? What time did it happen? It gets dark around four, right? He wouldn't be out in the dark. You knew I'd be at work until five, and you know I often stay late. I was there till nine o'clock, and not one phone call. Five whole hours you didn't try to call me. Don't you think I have a right to know? Kevin's *my child*. I'll be up on the next plane."

She rummaged through her purse for the dog-eared notebook that held her list of phone numbers. Airline. It was under *A*. She had never expected, before last summer, to go to Holland Mills again, and she hadn't filed the airline by its name.

A busy signal. She moaned in despair. After a moment she tried again. And again.

She dialed repeatedly for several minutes. It seemed an hour. When at last she heard it ring, she thought it must be a wrong number.

"I need a flight to Massena, New York," she told them. "It's an emergency. I don't care what time—"

"The flights are all booked, ma'am. We don't have anything before Friday."

"What?"

It was the holiday, they explained. Thanksgiving. It was the weather. For two days the northern airports had been closed and the connecting flights canceled because of fog.

"But my little boy's in the hospital. I *have* to get there."

"I'll see what I can do." It was a sympathetic voice. "I'll get back to you in a little while. Can you give me your number there?"

She gave the number. "Do you think there's any chance?"

"I'll see what I can do."

She walked aimlessly around the living room, the bedroom. She could not sit down.

Unconscious, her mother had said. For hours. What if he was brain damaged? What if he died?

She paced again. The waiting would kill her. She

5

couldn't handle this. It needed someone who would get tough with the airline.

Someone like—a man. They would listen to a man. It was unfair, but a fact of life, perhaps because women were raised from infancy to be more accommodating.

Except Ellen.

What more logical man was there than Travis Andrews?

No, she thought. Not Travis.

She didn't want to see him. And yet he had a stake in this. He was Kevin's father. And that was why she didn't want to see him. Because even now, after four years, he had no idea that he was Kevin's father. Or, for that matter, that Kevin existed.

She had no time to waste, but she needed to think about it. All of it.

She had been hurting when she met Travis. Again it was Ellen's fault. And Mike Corder's, and her parents'. And most of all, her own. She had needed someone like Travis. She needed the emotional solace, the approval, the physical closeness. But he hadn't been entirely free. He was in the process of getting a divorce, and then he left for a job in Brazil. He was gone before she knew about the baby. And perhaps Kevin was the important thing after all. Someone to whom she could belong and who belonged entirely to her.

Now Travis was home again. He had called her a few weeks ago and said he wanted to see her. She had told him she wasn't sure. She would have to think about it. And she had never called him back, which had been her intention all along, but she wasn't able to tell him that directly.

She felt sick at the idea of calling him now. He would be shocked by the whole thing. He would hate her, but she couldn't help it. She owed this much to Kevin.

Listening to the phone ring, she could feel her heart chugging slowly. She would think of Kevin. Only of Kevin.

"Travis?" The words came in a burst of fright. "It's Diane. Hastings. I need to talk to you. Are you free?"

"I'm free as a breeze. What's the problem?"

"Not on the phone. Can you come over? I can't tie up the phone, and I can't leave here."

Oh, God, it was not yet eleven. He probably had another woman there. But he had said he was free.

"Please, Travis? It's very important."

"I'll be there," he said. "I'll take a cab."

A cab. She felt enormously relieved, but the worst was still ahead. She pictured herself telling him. She rehearsed it. Never in her whole life had she done anything right. At least Ellen had been married when her baby was born. But it wasn't Kevin's fault. And he might need blood, and they didn't have any more—

The telephone rang. She stopped breathing.

The sympathetic voice of a few minutes earlier informed her, "I can get you a flight Thursday morning."

"But that's two days!"

A day and a half, actually.

"I'm sorry," she added more calmly, "I just can't wait that long."

"I'll see what I can do," the clerk said again. "You see, ma'am, everything's jammed up because of the airport closings and the holiday, but we'll try to get you something."

"Tomorrow, please? Tomorrow morning. Early."

The clerk said she would try. Diane thought she really would. She thought of all the happy travelers going somewhere for the holiday. She hated them.

The door buzzer sounded. Travis had gotten there in twenty minutes.

7

"Hey, good to see you!" He was smiling as he stepped off the elevator. "This isn't where you used to live, is it?"

"No, it's a sublet." She swallowed heavily. "Do you want to give me your coat? I'll hang it up."

His raincoat was damp. It was still drizzling outside. The damned weather.

He hadn't changed at all. Still the same tousled reddish-brown hair. Kevin had hair like that. Kevin had those bright blue eyes and even a faint dimple in his chin.

He said, "It's been a long time."

"Four years." Her voice came out a croak. "Travis, I— Why don't you sit down?"

She ought to have offered him a drink. For his sake. But she hadn't the patience for amenities. Everything in her was racing.

"Do you remember," she began, "we got sort of involved . . ."

"Sure I remember." He sounded surprised that she would ask. Then he seemed to realize what she might mean. "Hey, Diane—" And then again grew puzzled. She hadn't told him anything a month ago when they talked. He stopped trying to anticipate her and waited.

"I didn't know till after you left," she said. "I didn't try to get in touch with you. It didn't matter, and anyway, you were still married."

He understood. She could see it on his face. "He looks just like you," she added.

He had figured it out, but he hadn't adjusted. He tried to speak, cleared his throat, and tried again.

"Where is he? Did you—"

"I know it's a shock." She found herself starting to cry and hurried to the bathroom for a tissue.

"He's *supposed* to be here with me," she said as she

8

returned. "I raised him all by myself, and I worked, too. I hired nursemaids when he was little, and then I had him in a private day-care center. But last summer I got the flu. It turned into pneumonia. I was so sick I couldn't move. Finally I had to call my mother to come and help me. She took us both back to Holland Mills and gave up my apartment, so when I got well I had to leave him there till I found a place."

Travis nodded, still dazed. "I tried calling your old number. They said it was disconnected. That's why I called your office."

"He was with my sister," she said. "My parents both work. I got a call tonight. He was hit by a car. He's in the hospital, in a coma, and he might need more blood and they're all out of his type, which *I* have, so I could give it to him, but I can't get a flight. I just can't get one. I don't know what to do. Nobody ever listens to women. Could you please—*please* call the airline and yell and scream at them?"

He looked pained. She realized it was a reflection of her own pain. Then the usual Travis surfaced again.

"That's why they don't listen to women. Because women scream. You have to roar. Sound tough, not hysterical."

She handed him her address book. While he dialed and redialed, she said, "I hope you understand, I didn't call you just for this. I needed somebody. I can't—"

"Is he going to be all right?"

"I don't know. My mother didn't know. It happened this afternoon. They waited all that time before they called me. And my sister's so stupid. I never should have left him."

"Hello?"

She had known he could do it. Her hope flared and then dwindled as he talked.

"Is that what you got, too?" he asked, hanging up.

"It's the holiday and the fog," she explained. "All the airports up there were closed. I could take a train, but that's an all-day trip, and if he needs blood— I didn't mean to bother you about all this. I just had to talk to somebody, and I guess I don't really have anybody."

He rubbed his hand across his chin. "It's going to take me a while to get used to this, you know."

"I know."

"Wait a minute. Were you going to go all the way through life without telling me about him? Why do women think it only concerns them?"

"Well, biologically, I guess, it mostly does. And anyway, you were still married then."

"I'm not now. I haven't been for years."

"I didn't know how to reach you in Brazil."

She had known in the beginning, but he had moved around.

"Do you want to see a picture of him?" She opened her purse and took out her wallet.

He studied the picture in silence. Then he said, "You're right. He does look like me."

"You have a daughter, haven't you?"

"Yes. Shelley. She's in New Jersey with her mother."

"Travis, I don't know what to do. If the airline doesn't come through, is it quicker to rent a car or take the train?"

"Offhand, I don't know. How come you weren't going up there anyway for the holiday?"

The question took her by surprise. It made her feel guilty. A negligent mother.

"I don't get Friday off," she said, "and it's too far for just one day. Besides, I didn't think the holiday would mean much at his age, and I was going up anyway in a couple of weeks to get him. I found an apartment, and I'm moving the first of December."

"Congratulations."

She supposed he really meant it. Finding an apartment in New York City was cause for congratulations.

"It wasn't that I didn't want to see him," she went on, explaining herself. "It's just that, in a couple of weeks—"

She had already said it. And she couldn't bear thinking of it now, how she had looked forward to having him back.

"The reason I thought of it," he said, "is because I'm going up to Plattsburgh Thursday morning to see my folks."

She had forgotten that he came from Plattsburgh. It was on the eastern side of the Adirondacks, as Holland Mills was on the west. They had been introduced by a New Yorker of limited geographical vision, who exclaimed, "You two should get to know each other. You're practically neighbors!"

"I could have gotten a flight Thursday morning," she said. "I turned it down."

She realized as she spoke that it would have been better to keep it. She might end up with nothing.

"I'm getting an idea," Travis said. "I don't know if it'll work. We'll give the airline a little more time."

"What's your idea?"

"I could try to change my reservation to Wednesday—"

"But, Travis, you can't get a seat!"

"That's not what I'm talking about. I rented a plane. It comes out to more in the long run, since I'm staying till Sunday, but this is sort of a special thing for Shelley. We're going up together."

In a kaleidoscope of thoughts, she realized that his parents were Shelley's grandparents, and Kevin's, too.

She said, "I didn't know you could fly."

11

"Probably there are a lot of things we don't know about each other," he reminded her ruefully.

"Yes. I'm sorry. I really didn't think you'd care so much. And you already had Shelley."

"Your kid's part of me, too, isn't he?"

"I didn't think of it that way. I only thought of him as part of me."

He drew a deep breath that was almost a sigh. "I guess that's not too surprising."

Her fingernails dug into the arm of her chair. Everything she had ever done was wrong. Even depriving Travis of his child.

And that brought her back to where she had started. "Travis, what am I going to do?"

"Okay, here's what I had in mind. We'll wait and see what the airlines come up with, because that'll be the best and quickest way for you. If it's still negative, I'll try to get hold of Shelley in the morning, before school. Then I'll call the guy at the airport and see if I can change the plane for tomorrow. We'll fly you up to Massena, assuming the fog has cleared, then Shelley and I can go on to Plattsburgh. How does that sound?"

"You'd really do it? You'd go out of your way?"

"I thought you had to get there."

"I do!"

"I just want you to understand, there might be a problem with the plane. I rented a two-seater for Thursday, and I'll have to change that to a four-seater for Wednesday. Since there's a holiday, I might have trouble, but the guy I rent them from is an old pal. He'll try his best."

"Oh, thank God! Travis, I didn't know what I was going to do!"

She had never flown in a small plane. From the outside,

they were terrifyingly inadequate. But her fear had no place in this.

"You don't know what this does for me," she said. "If I couldn't get to him— I hope Shelley won't mind too much. Since it was supposed to be a treat for her."

"Mind missing a day of school? You want to bet?"

"How long will it take?"

"From New York to Massena? Maybe three or four hours."

Three or four hours. It would be direct, with no connecting flight. In four hours she could be in Massena. In another hour, at the hospital.

She would be there by early afternoon, if all went well.

3

North of Manhattan, just off Fordham Road in the Bronx, Jack's Fried Chicken was nearing its closing hour. Behind the counter a blond teenager named Becky Mercer packed what seemed like her millionth carton of crispy chicken. She stifled a yawn, covering it with the back of her hand because her fingers were greasy, and topped the carton with two buttered rolls.

From the next cash register, round-faced Gina Wallek, with the careful makeup job, gave her an amused smile. "Are we keeping you awake, hon?"

"It's been a long night," Becky replied.

"Every night's a long night. I don't know how you do it and go to school, too."

"I need the money."

"For what?"

"Christmas, and clothes, and things."

"I thought your old man was a cop," said Gina. "He must get pretty good pay."

Becky supposed it sounded good to a lot of people. "It gets spread pretty thin," she explained. "There's nine of us, including my parents." She handed the carton to a young couple who were talking in Spanish. "Enjoy your dinner."

The couple sat down at a table near the window. Becky turned to her next customer. "May I help you?"

He was tall and stoop-shouldered, with a knit cap pulled over his forehead. He peered at her curiously. "What are you doing here, Becky?"

"Oh, hi, Mr. Grady! Honestly, my next-door neighbor and I didn't even— I must be getting punchy. What time is it? Almost eleven?"

"Your folks let you work this late?" Mr. Grady asked. "Gimme a small bucket, honey. How long you been working here?"

"Three weeks. This is my third week. Yeah, the folks are on my back, but I need the money. It's just till Christmas."

"What, every night? You didn't quit school, did you?"

"Every night and Saturday, and I manage okay. School, too. Here you are, Mr. Grady. Enjoy."

Mr. Grady started toward the door but stepped aside as another customer pushed his way in. " 'Night, Becky. Take care of yourself."

Becky watched him leave. "I swear, Gina, you'd think two parents were enough, but I've got the whole neighborhood worrying about when I do my homework."

Gina was staring at the new customer. He was a slender man with a mustache and hard, dark eyes behind wire-rimmed glasses.

He backed against the wall. Gina gave an audible gasp as he reached inside his jacket. The next moment he was pointing a gun.

"Everybody stay right where you are. Just freeze."

They had already frozen. Hands raising chicken legs to mouths stopped in midair. The young Hispanic, reaching forward to protect his wife, remained halfway across the table.

"Down on the floor! Down on the floor!" The gunman's voice was shrill and metallic. "You," he told the girls behind the counter, "stay in sight and put up your hands."

Slowly, cautiously, the patrons lowered themselves to the floor. The gunman approached an elderly black man at one of the tables. "You, empty your pockets. Take off your pants. You, too," to the young couple. "Empty your pockets. Pockabook, jewlery. Make it quick. Take off your pants, and quick."

He sidled along the wall toward Gina. "Open the cash register, baby."

Gina gaped at him. He edged closer. She blinked rapidly and lifted a silver-tipped finger to the buttons on the register. Her hand began to tremble. A small, strangled noise came from her throat.

Becky turned to see if she needed help. The sudden motion, in her white-and-yellow uniform, caught the man's eye. He raised his gun and fired.

4

Two fellow officers went to notify Becky's family. It was late at night, but the Mercers had not gone to bed. They always waited up for Becky. Now big, gray-haired Gerald Mercer, in his pajamas and bathrobe, sat slumped in an armchair, a hand across his eyes.

"She was only a kid. Only sixteen," he said over and over again. "Why'd he have to shoot her for?"

His wife, Doris, moved about in a trance. She insisted upon making coffee for the two visitors, clutching as best she could at normality.

"It was her first job," Jerry said. "She wanted the money for Christmas."

He had seen it before, lots of times in nineteen years on the force. He'd had to break the news to families, but he never thought it would be his own kid.

Maybe it wasn't. Maybe there was hope yet. If he willed it hard enough, he could make this night go back where it came from and never happen. He *could* do it. There had to be a way.

"Anyhow," said his buddy Norman Lucas, who had been the one to tell him, which made Norman wish he had kept to his old career of selling shoes, "we got a good description. That Wallek girl froze when he told her to open the register, but she's got eyes. Didn't miss a thing. The guy's a white man, about six feet tall. Well built, with gold-rimmed glasses, dark hair, mustache, wearing a navy-blue knit cap and a brown corduroy jacket with elbow patches."

"She noticed all that?" exclaimed the other policeman, although it was scarcely news to him. "She's a witness in a million. Ten million." They both glanced at Jerry, wondering if he had even heard them.

"He didn't have to kill her," Jerry told the window. "He shouldn't have killed my girl."

Doris, having made and served the coffee, sat down in the chair next to his. A dazed expression came over her face. She fumbled in the pocket of her bathrobe for a handkerchief.

Later that night Jerry heard another report. Unrelated. Maybe. He hadn't been able to sleep. He lay slumped in the armchair with the radio on. Round-the-clock news. Voices. It made him feel less alone.

On Broadway at 207th Street, in Manhattan's Thirty-fourth Precinct, two policemen had been shot dead. Witnesses saw a man fleeing the scene. A slender Caucasian wearing glasses and a tan coat.

He sat up straight, his eyes wide open. Two of them. Two at once. Jesus Holy Christ.

But that was not really what got him. It was the glasses.

Nothing else checked out. Only the glasses. And an uncanny, unexplained feeling in his gut.

Farther south, Travis Andrews poured them each a glass of sherry. It was all Diane had available.

She set hers on the coffee table. She couldn't touch it. "It doesn't seem right to be drinking."

"I don't know about you," Travis replied, "but I need it. I just became the father of a three-year-old kid who's

18

smashed up in the hospital. You couldn't have broken it to me gradually."

"I didn't know how." She bit down on her tears. "And there's something else you're going to kill me for."

He shook his head, trying to rid himself of the daze. "Tell me. I'll let you know if it's a capital crime."

"You see, there wasn't any way I could—well, you'd have to understand about my family. And me."

"You told them you were married."

She looked away quickly. Of course he had guessed. What else was there?

"I used your name," she went on, glancing at him and then away again, as though he were blinding, like the sun. "I even used it on Kevin's birth certificate. It's his name. Kevin Andrews."

"Not a bad name."

"You don't mind?"

"It's fait accompli, isn't it?"

He did mind. She concentrated on her glass of sherry.

He moved closer, resting his arm across the back of the sofa, almost touching her shoulders.

"It's okay, Diane." He sounded tired. "I just don't know if it's legal."

"I don't know, either," she mumbled.

"Now tell me what happened."

"About the accident? I don't know. He was in the driveway. She wasn't watching him."

"Your sister?"

"She never did learn to take responsibility. But it wouldn't have happened to her own kid, I know that."

"Who hit him?"

"A car went in to turn around. Ellen didn't know he was anywhere near it till she saw him lying there."

"Ellen's your sister?"

"Please. I'd rather not think about Ellen."

"I don't see how you can avoid it."

Nor did she. If it hadn't been for Ellen's carelessness— In fact, her whole life would have been different, if it hadn't been for Ellen.

"Drink up," said Travis, "and then get some sleep."

"What about you?"

"I'll borrow your sofa, if that's okay. It beats going home."

"You can have the bed. And, Travis—"

"The sofa's just fine."

"Travis, I'm sorry. About everything. And I really didn't mean you had to help me get there. I just—needed someone."

"No problem," he said.

She provided him with a blanket and a pillow, and then went to her bedroom, leaving the door ajar so she could hear if the telephone rang. She lay down on the bed and pulled a blanket over her. She did not expect to sleep.

From the street came the sounds of traffic, tires on wet pavement. She saw the room faintly in a glow from the window.

All those hours. If she had known sooner, she might have gotten a flight. Or at least a train or a bus. She'd have been there in the morning.

She shouldn't have left him. Kevin was her whole world. She had failed him, as she failed at everything else. At being a daughter, a lover, a mother. It was always she who failed, while Ellen succeeded.

5

Diane had been four years old when Ellen was born. She was old enough to realize there was something sudden and frightening about the event, but not old enough to know what it was. Only later did she understand that Ellen had been a "preemie," born nearly three months too soon. It was a long time before they could be sure that Ellen would live.

She still remembered that winter morning and the time afterward when her mother was gone from home. Then her mother came back, and sometime later there was talk about a baby. Mysteriously, she had a sister somewhere. They told her she could take care of the new baby. And it would be a playmate for her.

She looked forward to having a sister she could play with. When at last she saw the baby, her disappointment was enormous. Nobody could play with a thing like that. It was even more fragile than a doll. She was barely allowed to touch the baby, and no one could sneeze or cough in its presence.

Besides, it didn't have any hair. It was a useless, scrawny, bald-headed object that cried shrilly and often.

But it was her baby sister. They had said she could help take care of the baby. One time when Ellen was crying, Diane pulled a chair over to the crib, climbed up and tried to lift her out.

A shriek from the doorway made her drop the baby and nearly fall off her chair. Clinging to the edge of the crib, she looked around, terrified.

Her mother rushed toward her. "Diane, don't *ever* touch the baby again. You could hurt her very badly. What on earth did you think you were doing?"

Diane was too frightened to answer. She had never seen her mother so angry. Besides, although she had meant no harm, she could well understand that it would be a terrible thing to hurt the baby. While her mother comforted Ellen, Diane went to her own room and lay on her bed, staring at the wall.

Not long after she came home from the hospital, Ellen began developing from a bald, fetal object into a plump and lively baby. Her eyes remained blue and her hair grew out in silvery blond curls. People exclaimed that she was adorable.

Soon Diane formed a picture of what "adorable" meant. It meant small and helpless, as opposed to "our big girl." Curly blond fluff, rather than brown hair that grew straight and thick. Clear, blue eyes, like the sky, instead of muddy green. It meant a tiny hand reaching for a finger, a tiny achievement, such as rolling over or sitting up. It meant a single tooth appearing overnight. She was not able to understand that anything Ellen did seemed remarkable when, for such a long time, Ellen's very survival had been in doubt.

Ellen continued to survive and thrive and later on, to blossom. In the early years, Diane was aware only of a vague discomfort. Ellen didn't mean to be small and frail, or even pretty and charming.

Up to a point.

There came a time—Diane was not sure at what moment it happened but only that it had happened—when suddenly Ellen did mean it. And Diane seemed to be the only one who noticed. Ever.

Diane was seventeen by the time she had her first real boyfriend. He was Donald Blake, a member of the basketball team and a trumpet player in the school band. He was attractive, sought-after, and had actually chosen Diane.

At first she avoided telling her family, afraid that they would tease her. There was no way they could find out, as long as she and Don met only after school.

But then, at the end of the basketball season, there was a Saturday night dance. Don assumed they would go together. She assumed so, too. She waited until the afternoon of the dance to inform her mother that she would need an early dinner because she was going out.

She had not meant for Ellen to hear, but Ellen did. "Wow, it's about time," she exclaimed. "I thought you were turning into an old maid. Who's the guy?"

"Somebody named Donald Blake."

"*Don Blake?*" Ellen's eyes opened wide. She knew who he was. She knew all of them. The school was so small that the seventh and eighth grades were in the same building as the high school.

Ellen's interest gave Diane her first wave of apprehension. It didn't matter that Ellen was only a child. Ellen didn't feel like a child and she didn't look like one, in her eyeliner and tight-fitting jeans.

Diane said, "We're leaving at seven, so I have to eat early."

She did not think she would be able to eat at all. As it turned out, she couldn't.

And as it turned out, she had been right about Ellen. As

23

soon as Don arrived, Ellen made an entrance down the stairs. She pretended surprise. Her face lit up. "Oh, *hi!*" she exclaimed and turned on a lethal flood of charm while Diane stood awkwardly buttoning and unbuttoning her coat.

As they left the house, he asked about Ellen. How old was she?

"Thirteen," Diane said scathingly. "I told you she's my kid sister."

"She sure doesn't look like a kid."

"Well, she is. Take my word for it."

"I wasn't arguing."

They settled into silence as he drove toward the school. After a while, not knowing what made her say it, she remarked, "I can still remember Ellen when she was born. She didn't have any hair, and she was so skinny and ugly."

"There's been a few changes," he said.

"They didn't think she'd live. She was premature and she had something wrong with her heart. It's no wonder she was so skinny. You should have seen her, she looked like a newborn rat."

Diane had never seen a newborn rat, but it sounded like a good comparison.

"Yeah, well . . ."

She wished she hadn't said that about Ellen. She had made herself seem small and vindictive.

It isn't Ellen's fault. She closed her eyes tightly in the darkness of the car. *It isn't Ellen's fault she almost died.*

Or mine, either.

She had thought college would be different. A new beginning. At college she met Mike Corder, and they were together for most of their junior year. He told her she was beautiful. No one had ever told her that before. She, in turn, responded to his mischievous smile and rugged rang-iness, which was not handsome but rather endearingly awkward. As the spring semester came to an end, he sug-gested that next year they take an apartment together off campus.

"No, Mike," she said as they lay side by side under a tree, "I just can't do that. I don't want to get involved yet. Not that way."

She did not need to explain. In his own words she had been holding him off ever since they met. From time to time he would praise her as something special. At other times her abstinence made him frustrated and angry. He accused her of teasing him.

"I'm not teasing," she retorted. "You should know me by now, but you keep giving me a hard time about it."

"You're not giving me a hard time?" He looked pained. "What are we going to do, Diane?"

She did not reply. After a moment or two, he said, "Don't you think we're too young to get married?"

"Of course we are. But maybe next year, after we graduate, we wouldn't be."

"Is that what you want?"

"This isn't very romantic, Mike."

"What should I do? Get down on my knees?"

She laughed. He was already supine on the grass.

And so they became engaged—unofficially, but as far as she was concerned, it was enough. She felt as though they were almost married. Until they actually were, however, she intended to "wait." Or, as he put it, "hold out." He told her she was driving him crazy. At the same time he ad-mitted that he rather liked it.

"It's old-fashioned, but it's nice," he said, "saving yourself like that. And practical, I guess. After all, what if you got pregnant and I got hit by a car?"

"Or changed your mind."

He was shocked. "I wouldn't change my mind, Di. I love you too much."

During the summer they wrote to each other from their respective jobs and missed each other desperately. In September he drove to Holland Mills to give her a ride back to college.

Her parents were favorably impressed by him. "Down-to-earth" was how Marian Hastings described him. She was pleased by his interest in business administration. "I wonder, Firman," she said to her husband, "if there might be something he could do at the mill after graduation."

"That's the family business," Diane explained to Mike. "They make knitwear."

"I'm sure we could find something," Diane's father agreed. "It would be entry level, of course, but there would definitely be a future in management. Would you be interested, young man?"

"And then," Marian added with a smile, "we wouldn't be losing our daughter."

Mike declined to commit himself until he had seen the mill, the executive offices, and had gotten an idea of what he might be doing and what he could expect for his future. He concluded that it seemed quite promising. He liked the town, he liked the mill, and he liked Diane's family. It would be a terrific place to start, he said.

In the two days Mike stayed at their house, he and Ellen became quite good friends. They developed a light, teasing relationship. In Ellen's case Diane thought of it as flirting.

She tried to tell herself she was being unfair, but she knew she wasn't. Even though Mike was not particularly handsome, he had an attractiveness of his own, and Ellen had never been one to pass up an attractive man.

Especially, Diane thought bitterly, *my attractive men.*

But why, she wondered, when there were certainly enough to go around? *Why mine? It's almost as if she does it on purpose.*

When they were finally in Mike's car on their way back to college, he grinned suddenly and shook his head. "That sister of yours sure is a lively one."

Diane leaned back against the headrest and gazed at the road. "She always acts like that when there are men around."

"She's cute. How old is she?"

"Seventeen, going on three."

Again she was ashamed of herself, not because the remark was undeserved but because it made her seem a jealous clod compared with Ellen.

And once again she told herself: But I am a jealous clod. That's exactly what I am.

As the school year progressed, Mike seemed to forget about Ellen. Out of sight, out of mind. For the first time in her life, Ellen started writing to Diane. She wrote twice a week, sometimes oftener, chatty letters giving news of home and friends, and always closing with the request: "Give my love to Mike." Diane never did. She managed, as much as possible, to avoid mentioning Ellen at all to Mike.

During the spring vacation, Mike went home with her to Holland Mills, so they could begin looking for a place to live. They found a small house for rent on a country road only a mile from the mill.

She spent the holiday making arrangements for their wedding and reception and shopping for house furnishings.

27

It would have been fun if Mike had joined her in planning their home, but he was not really interested. He told her he wanted to spend some time at the mill, learning what he could about its operation and his future responsibilities there.

She did not know how much time he actually put in at the mill, but he always seemed to be at her parents' home when she returned from her errands. Ellen, too, was there. Diane felt her old familiar pain every time she saw them together, for their friendship had resumed where it left off, but she tried not to give it much thought. She would only aggravate herself and perhaps even plant ideas in their heads.

The day before they were to return to school, she noticed that Mike and Ellen seemed to be avoiding each other. She wondered if they had had a fight. And if so, what they had to fight about.

In addition, Ellen was quite moody that day. Maybe that had caused the disagreement. When Diane began telling Mike about a carpet pattern she had liked, Ellen turned with a gasping sob and ran up the stairs.

"What's the matter with her?" Diane asked.

"She's okay," said Mike. "You know how kids are. She'll be all right."

Diane wondered why he was so quick to reassure her. She had not been the least bit worried about Ellen, only curious.

She decided Ellen must have had a crush on Mike, and mention of the carpet had brought home to her the fact that he was not to be hers.

Two months later, Diane remembered that thought. How stupid could she have been?

They let her graduate before they told her. At least they

gave her that much. The blow fell a few hours later when they all went to dinner at the Manor Arms, an inn near the college. It was supposed to be a happy occasion. She wondered why they decided to tell her then.

As if she couldn't guess. They wanted to be sure she was in a large and elegant dining room full of people, so she wouldn't make a scene. What they expected from her, she never knew.

"Diane," her mother began, when they were halfway through a round of drinks, "I realize this is going to be hard for you, when you've made your plans and all, but it's something you have to know. The sooner the better, I think."

Apprehensively Diane looked around at the circle of faces. Her mother's head was tilted to one side, her expression sad and sympathetic. Her father watched her, frowning slightly. Mike was intent upon his water goblet as he rocked it around on its base. Ellen, her face white and pinched, sat with her head bowed, staring at the table.

"Nobody meant it to happen," Marian went on in a gentle tone. "You have to understand that, dear. It's just a terribly unfortunate thing. Ellen—" And Ellen's mouth tightened still further. "Ellen's going to have a baby."

Diane glanced again at Ellen and wondered what the fuss was about. Surely they weren't so uptight that they thought this was anything unusual. Or were they trying to tell her that Ellen's marriage would have to take precedence over her own?

Mike tried to speak, found he had no voice, and tried again. "It's my baby, Di," he said, never taking his eyes from the water glass.

Her lips parted. She said the first thing that came to her mind. "How do you know?"

29

He turned his head and looked at her sideways. "Because I know." There was a trace of anger in his voice.

He loves her, Diane thought. She felt suddenly very heavy and very cold. She felt like a lump of stone.

From far off, her mother was saying, "I know you'll understand. Mike wants to do right by Ellen."

Briefly Diane remembered all the times he had begged her to make their love, in his words, "the real thing." Complete. And he claimed to respect her for wanting to wait. But Ellen had been there, ready and easy.

Again her eyes swept over her parents' faces. Didn't they realize— Didn't any of them realize what Ellen was?

She turned to her sister, who still refused to look at her.

"Little whore," Diane said and got up from the table.

She was aware of people staring as she swept through the dining room. She didn't care. She reached the front desk and asked the clerk to call a taxi. Her heart pounded and the lobby spun drunkenly. She felt her mother come up beside her, heard her mother's voice begging her to understand, to forgive, and show how big she could be, to come back with her now and not spoil the dinner.

"Wouldn't dream of spoiling it," Diane said. She rested her hands on the desk and gazed emptily at the mail slots until the taxi arrived. Her last glimpse was of Marian standing on the steps of the inn watching her drive away.

She asked the taxi to take her back to the college, where her possessions were packed and ready to go. Beyond that she could not think.

A powder-blue station wagon stood in front of the dorm. Pamela Rhinehart, her roommate. Pam would see her, but it was too late to hide. Diane fought back tears and humiliation as she climbed out of the taxi.

In a blur she saw Pam coming toward her. *Diane, what's the matter? Are you crying? What happened?*

Unable to hold it back, Diane sobbed out the story. They all heard it, Pam's whole family. They rearranged the station wagon to make room for Diane's luggage.

As she carried out her carton of books, a flash of green appeared on the slope above the campus. She felt gratified. They were coming. They would see how she was managing.

It was her father and Mike. They wanted her to come back. Mike pleaded with her to understand. She thought it was a stupid thing to say and could not think of a fitting answer. Her father asked where they were taking her. Mr. Rhinehart handed him a business card, saying, "It's on there." She felt worse for her father than for Mike. And she wondered what was wrong with her that the whole thing had happened to begin with. Something was wrong. Even her parents had sided with Ellen. But that was not so unusual.

The Rhineharts lived on a quiet street in New Rochelle, just outside New York City. Diane stayed with them until she found a job and a place of her own.

She was a trainee in a Wall Street brokerage house. She could scarcely believe her luck. Money had always fascinated her. The job and the little apartment in Manhattan would never have been hers, she reminded herself, if she had married Mike and stayed in Holland Mills.

But even that didn't help very much. It didn't make her forgive her family. Or Mike. Or herself. Once she cried to Pam, "It's all my fault. He kept wanting to make love—you know, go all the way—and I wouldn't let him. I thought we should wait. I really thought—"

"It's not your fault," Pam replied firmly. "It's Mike's and Ellen's fault, so quit taking it out on yourself."

It was sensible advice, but Diane could not help thinking that it all might have turned out differently if *she* had been different.

A week after the episode at Manor Arms, Mike and Ellen were married. Again her mother begged Diane to forgive them and at least write Ellen a note. Diane, still at a loss for an adequate comment, did not reply.

On her job she met other trainees, many of them single young men. She wanted nothing to do with them.

"Don't you know how lucky you are?" Pam asked her over lunch one day. "In my office they're all married, gay, or generally weird. You have it made."

Diane did not have anything made. Her entire life had been undone, and she was still trying to understand it.

She finally accepted a date with a man named Anthony, who worked in another department. They went to dinner and then to a French movie on Eighth Street. She was preoccupied the whole time, wondering what she would do when he took her home. She was sick of being a virgin. Saving herself for what? It had all turned out a mockery.

When they reached her door, she invited him in for a glass of wine. If she hadn't, he probably would have suggested it anyway. She could tell he was interested, and that made her despise him. In setting his sights on her, he had set them too low.

After the second glass he began to stroke her leg. He was slow but steady, working his way up to her turtleneck sweater, which he attempted to remove. She clutched at it fiercely.

"Relax," he said. "What do you think I am?"

A gorilla. It flashed through her mind that, all along, she had been not so much chaste as afraid.

She would have to face it sooner or later if she was to join the human race. "Can I turn the light out?" she asked.

"Sure, if you want to. It's your light."

She felt a little better when he couldn't see her. A little

more in control when she removed her own clothes instead of letting him undress her. There was no preliminary caress. Probably she would not have welcomed it if there had been. As he forced himself upon her, she drew back, whimpering.

"Relax," he said again, this time angrily.

She could not relax. And yet she wanted it over with. She wanted to be initiated so she wouldn't have to go through it again. But this was all wrong.

Anthony gave up. Lashing out at her with frustrated insults, he pulled on his clothes and left the apartment.

She tried to tell herself that it was his fault for being so brutish, yet she knew it was hers, too. But she couldn't help it. And when she thought of Ellen, who had done it so easily and naturally, she hated herself all the more.

6

In the middle of the night, Ellen was wrenched from her sleep by someone calling her. A soft voice next to her bed.

"Mommy! What happened to Kevin?"

"Ssh!" whispered Ellen, raising her head. "You'll wake Daddy." She listened. He was still sound asleep.

"But what happened?"

"Kevin got hurt. They took him to the hospital so he can get well."

"Did our car hurt him?"

Oh God, thought Ellen.

At the garden, across the lawn. Examining the flowers. And it had been getting dark.

"No, sweetie. A car came into the driveway to turn around. They didn't see Kevin."

"What car?"

"A—just a big car. An old one."

"Why didn't you tell them?"

"I didn't *know*. Remember, I was busy with the groceries. Now go on back to bed before you wake Daddy. He needs his sleep."

"Is Kevin going to die?"

"He is not. Why do you ask such a dumb question?"

Go! Go!

But Natalie remained by the bed, her face a pale moon in the darkness. Ellen could almost see her frowning as she tried to puzzle it out.

She was only four years old. You could keep telling her over and over again. After a while she'd think she remembered another car.

"Mommy, when the ambliance came, was Kevin dead?"

"He was *not*. I told you. Now will you go back to your room?"

"I want to get in bed with you and Daddy."

"No, baby." She couldn't take it. Her nerves were already screaming.

"But I want to."

Her voice rose. If Natti got too wrought up, she might blurt something. But why now? Why couldn't she leave them alone?

Grudgingly, Ellen moved over and let her daughter climb into the bed. As she pressed against him, Mike stirred and mumbled something. He did that sometimes, mumbled in his sleep. She never heard what he said, but she was always afraid it would be "Diane."

To Diane, it seemed as though the night had just begun. She did not feel that she had slept at all, but the room had lightened to a medium gray.

The door was still partly open. She heard Travis's voice. "Yes, we'll be here. Anything you can do. Thanks."

She got up and went out to the living room. "I heard you just now. It's still hopeless, right?"

He said, "Look, it's not even daylight. Give them a chance. They can't do much between midnight and six A.M."

She hadn't heard the phone ring. "Then why did you call them?"

"Because I'm as fidgety as you are. Do you know what this does to a guy?"

She knew what it did to her. She found it hard to believe that Travis could feel the same way.

He said, "In a little while I'll try to get my daughter and then Bill Adams."

"You don't have to do this, you know," she burst out angrily. The whole thing was getting to her. She hadn't meant to take it out on him, but he was just there.

"I know," he said. "I'm doing it for the boy, not for you."

She wanted to tell him she was sorry, but she couldn't. Instead, she pictured herself actually on a plane. A real one, not a small rented toy. She did not know why it had to be so difficult.

Travis said, "I think I'll go home and grab a few clothes, in case we end up with Plan B. You'll be here to get the phone, won't you?"

"Where else?" she asked.

While he was gone, she packed a bag of her own. She had not thought of it last night. She waited for the phone to ring. She dreaded it, too, another call from Holland Mills. It could only be worse news. The phone remained silent.

Travis was back in less than an hour. He told her he had talked to his daughter.

"She'll meet us at the airport, unless she hears from me."

"She really doesn't mind this?"

"If she does, she didn't say so. I'm going to call Jersey, okay? I couldn't get Bill Adams before."

While he made the call, she brewed a pot of coffee. His conversation was brief. She could hear it from the kitchen. She had steeled herself for bad news when Travis announced, "He thinks he might have a plane, but he won't know for sure till he gets to the office."

36

"So what do we do?"

"We proceed on the assumption that he has one. Anyhow, there are other places. I'm going to try the airline one more time, then we'll give it up."

He called and gave up, muttering, "I don't see why they can't just bump somebody."

She prepared a breakfast of scrambled eggs and toast while he studied his aviation charts.

"You're going to have to help me with this," he told her. "Since both of us want to be on our way, I won't spend a lot of time on it now. Pull your chair over and I'll show you briefly, so at least you'll know what we're talking about. Shelley can help, too, but she's only a kid."

She moved closer so that she could see the chart he had spread out on the table. It was a confusing mass of colors, figures, and concentric circles.

"This is where we start. I hope." He pointed to an X'd dot in the heart of a large yellow splotch, which she recognized as the New York metropolitan area. "The first part's easy. We'll fly up the Hudson River to Albany. Then we head over the Adirondacks, and that's going to be a little more complicated. I'll need landmarks for that. Everything that shows on the chart. Lakes, rivers, mountains, even cabins."

With a felt-tip pen he traced their line of flight. "Got that? We'll work on it some more on the way over."

"If you don't need me right now, I'm going to call the hospital," she said.

It was early morning and the offices at the hospital were not fully staffed. It took a minute or so to reach someone who could help her. They told her there had been no change in Kevin's condition.

"Do you mean he's still in a coma?" she cried.

37

"That's all I can tell you right now," was the answer.

Travis looked up from his charts. "That's better than it could be," he said.

The remark annoyed her. What did Kevin mean to him? He didn't even know Kevin.

More questions tumbled through her mind. Was Kevin really alive? If there had been brain death, would they tell her over the phone? Would her mother have told her? She would have to get there quickly and take charge.

But Travis was not ready to leave. He listened to the radio, telephoned for a weather report, and figured things on a pocket computer. Diane sipped her coffee and stared out of the window. The clouds were gone and the sun was shining. Good flying weather. If only they could get started.

She looked over at Travis and remembered the night they met. It was a party on the East Side. One of her college friends. How come they all ended up in New York?

In the first five minutes, she learned that Travis was an engineer and had applied for a job in Brazil. That he had a wife, but they were getting divorced. Nothing about him at that time was available or permanent. Perhaps that was why her guard stayed down. He was not looking for a wife or even a lay. While they talked, she sipped a bloody mary. By the time he offered to take her home, she was feeling free and adventurous.

At her apartment they had another round of drinks. "I'm on a bloody mary kick," she told him as she sat down on his knee. She had never been so bold with a man. Or so light-hearted. They felt relaxed with each other. He was not compulsively out for sex, and she did not care about attracting him. It made it that much easier when they moved into the bedroom.

Travis was very different from Anthony. He was gentle, unpressured, and caring. And he succeeded where Anthony had failed. When it was over, she felt that a great hurdle had been overcome. She did not want him to leave her. Ever.

But he did. And she was still unsatisfied. Yet she was satisfied, too, because she had done it. Finally. She was a real woman now. At twenty-one. While Ellen—

Like everything else in life, it had come so easily to Ellen.

Travis looked up from his charts. "Ready to go?" She was surprised at the question. She had been ready since last night.

Quickly she rinsed the dishes and put on her goose-down jacket for the trip north. When they left the building, she found that, in spite of the sunshine, the air had turned crisp and cool. A gusty wind blew along the avenue, swirling bits of trash and a few dry leaves.

"What happens if there's a lot of turbulence?" she asked.

"This isn't bad. We might get buffeted a little, but it's not a problem."

She felt something like a mushroom cloud rise up in her chest, ready to explode. She did not want to ride in a tiny, light plane, bouncing and shaking in the wind. She didn't want Kevin to be near death. Her whole life was out of control.

The cloud did not explode, but it was still there as they descended the steps into the subway and boarded a train for the bus terminal at the George Washington Bridge.

7

It was after nine by the time they reached Teterboro Airport. She would have to call her office.

"Are you cold?" he asked. He was sorry he didn't have a car. It was a long walk from the bus stop.

"No," she said, her teeth chattering. "I'm okay. Just nervous."

"About the flight or the kid?"

"Both, I guess."

"Don't worry about the flight. As long as I keep my eyes open, you can close yours."

He brightened suddenly and waved to something down the road. A gray car had drawn up beside a small white trailer. A figure jumped out of the car and waved back excitedly.

He began to walk faster. She hoped the car would leave. She did not want to meet Travis's ex-wife, but of course Pat would stay with her daughter, at least until she could turn her over to Daddy.

As they approached, a blonde in a pink quilted coat stepped from the car.

"Pat," said Travis, "I'd like you to meet Diane Hastings. This is Pat uh—Brophy, Diane. And my daughter, Shelley."

"Nice to meet you," Diane said. They both murmured something. Pat was uninterested, Shelley downright hostile. He had said she wouldn't mind. It seemed she did, but that didn't matter. Nothing mattered except getting to Kevin as soon as possible.

Shelley was tall for twelve years old and had the same reddish hair that Kevin had inherited. Hers was a few shades lighter. Her face was sweet, heart-shaped, and sprinkled with freckles.

Pat said, "I hope you know what you're doing, Travis. I don't see why a regular flight wouldn't have done just as well."

"Diane here has been trying to get a regular flight since last night," Travis told her. "There aren't any, even for a lady in distress. That's why we're leaving today instead of tomorrow."

"Well, be careful."

"Oh, Mom," Shelley exclaimed. "Daddy has two hundred sixty hours."

Pat made a face that implied she was not impressed by the record. "You couldn't take a commercial flight for the return?"

"I think," he said, "they'll expect us to bring back the plane. Which reminds me, I'd better see what he's got."

A sign over the trailer door said Adams Aviation, Rentals, Leasing, Charter, Instruction. Inside, a square-faced man rose from behind a large steel desk and shook Travis's hand.

"Got one for ya. It's a Skylane. And I have a passenger for the fourth seat, if you're interested."

"A what?" asked Travis.

"Skylane."

"A passenger?"

Only then did he notice the man waiting quietly on a bench against the wall. An unobtrusive man, wearing sunglasses and a raincoat that seemed too big for him. A bright blue nylon duffel bag rested on the bench beside him.

The man stood up. "I don't want to put you to any trouble sir, but I heard you were heading up north, and I've got to get to Montreal."

"We're only going to Massena," Travis said, "and then Plattsburgh."

"If you wouldn't mind. I could catch a bus from there. It's my wife. They took her to the hospital. It's very bad, and I— Business hasn't been too good, and I—"

"Oh—" Diane gasped.

He went on, nervously wetting his lips. "I'll pay what I can. I'll send you the rest later."

"Oh, Travis," said Diane.

Travis was scowling. "This is very unusual. And I'm not licensed to take paying passengers."

"But, Travis, his wife. How else is he going to get there?"

The square-faced man, who was evidently Bill Adams, said, "If you kept it to expenses . . ."

"Would that make it legal?" asked the man in the raincoat. He was tense, waiting.

"I know exactly how you feel," Diane sympathized. "My little boy is in a hospital near Massena."

Travis said, "Let me check," and went outside.

Of course. Poor Shelley.

A moment later he returned. "I guess it'll be okay, as far as Massena. You'll have to get yourself to Montreal from there."

While Travis handled the paperwork, Diane found a pay phone and called their respective offices. And then a collect call to her parents' home. She had to know how he was, whether he had regained consciousness.

42

There was no answer. They had probably left for the mill. Or the hospital. She thought of trying Ellen's house, but didn't know the number. She did not want to talk to Ellen. In a few hours she would be there with him. Four hours. He might even be awake by then.

When she went back to the desk, Shelley was there. In Shelley's face and coloring she saw Kevin. She had not noticed before how long Shelley's hair was. Almost down to her waist. "You have beautiful hair," Diane told her.

Shelley responded with a chilly "Thanks." She was probably accustomed to being told she had beautiful hair. Still, it was almost the only beautiful thing about her. Except for her eyes. She had the potential for being a very striking woman, but was late in blooming. Because of her height, it was hard to remember that she was only twelve. Diane, too, had been awkward at that age. Hopelessly ugly, she had felt.

She tried again. "I appreciate your letting me come along. It really is an emergency. My little boy was in a bad accident, and I couldn't get a regular flight."

"It's okay." Shelley moved close to her father, who was studying the plane's manual. It seemed to take forever. Diane had not realized how much needed to be done beforehand. There were more computations on the calculator. Another lengthy study of the charts. It was no wonder he had told her that the airline would be quicker.

Finally after a phone call or two, he was ready. They went out a back door onto the field, where rows of small planes rocked in the wind, straining at their mooring cables. They looked like giant insects. That was all. Just insects. The only thing substantial about them would be the weight of the passengers.

Shelley walked ahead with her father. Diane and the stranger followed. His head was down, his shoulders hunched. Diane shivered in the wind that blew across the vast, flat field. "Do you know if planes have heaters?" she asked.

He looked up, frowning behind the sunglasses. "Most likely. I don't know a lot about it."

Of course they would. They flew at altitudes even colder than the ground. She hoped he wouldn't think of that and decide she was an idiot.

"I didn't catch your name," she said. "Mine's Diane Hastings."

"Dearborn, okay? Arnold Dearborn."

"Do you come from Montreal?"

"No. New York. My wife was visiting up there. Her sister. Married a fella from up there."

"It must have been horrible when you heard she was sick. I hope everything's going to be all right."

"Yeah, me too."

Travis stopped beside a blue-and-white plane.

"This seems to be it. You folks might as well get in and stay out of the wind. I have to check it over."

He opened one of the doors. The luggage went in first, to a space in back of the seats. Then Diane and Arnold Dearborn climbed into the rear seat and Shelley into the front. Diane watched Travis prowling about, peering into the fuel tanks. As she turned her head, her eyes met those of her companion. She looked away quickly. His sunglasses disconcerted her. It occurred to her that maybe he had been crying. Or drinking, although she couldn't smell anything. She noticed a tiny nick on his upper lip. He must have cut himself while shaving.

She asked, "What made you try the airport? That was taking quite a chance, wasn't it, hoping to find somebody going your way. Have you done it before?"

44

"I didn't know what else to do," he said. "I coulda hitched a ride in a car, but do you know how long it takes to get to Montreal?"

"Yes, I do. And a lot of people won't pick up hitchhikers, anyway."

He shrugged. "You can usually get something." He ran his finger across his upper lip, feeling the nick. Then he asked, "Has this man done a lot of flying?"

Shelley turned from the front seat. "Two hundred sixty hours."

"Well, I wouldn't know," he said. "Is that a lot?"

"It's enough." Shelley sounded indignant. "It's better than a lot of people."

Travis climbed into the plane and latched the doors. The man leaned forward.

"You have two hundred sixty hours' flying time?"

"That's right," said Travis. "What about it?"

"He wants to know if that's enough, Daddy," Shelley said, with a baleful look at their passenger.

Travis was unruffled. "It's okay for a trip like this, as long as we don't run into weather problems. I haven't got instrument rating."

"You don't think there's going to be weather problems?"

"No, I checked everything. The rain and fog are out at sea. There's a cold front coming in, but we should be at Massena by then and hopefully Plattsburgh."

"What's the problem with a cold front? Snow?"

"Icing."

Travis was checking the instruments. Another wait. Diane fastened her seat belt. She looked up at the latch that held the doors. It seemed secure, but she was unconvinced. What was to prevent it from opening and spilling them all out? She wanted to ask if people ever fell out of

45

small planes, but she didn't dare. She had never heard of it happening.

He switched on the power. She could *hear* it, a crescendoing whine. Then the engine. The plane began to quiver. Travis was talking into the radio, asking for takeoff instructions.

The inside of the plane was cold, padded in beige plastic. Cold and insubstantial.

But it was taking her to Kevin. She saw herself walking into his room. Saw his face light up at the sight of her. He wouldn't still be unconscious, he couldn't be, after a whole night.

Suddenly they were moving. *My God, we're moving.* Taxiing toward the runway.

She settled down into herself. Made her mind go numb. There was more exchange on the radio. And the plane sat, waiting.

Then it began to hurtle forward, jouncing and trembling, picking up speed. It would shake to pieces. She closed her eyes and opened them to see the ground falling away. The trees and buildings sank out of sight. They were airborne.

8

Ellen Corder sat beside her mother in the fourth-floor lounge at the hospital. At any moment she expected Diane to come rushing in, her face distraught, the tragic heroine.

Natalie was at home with a baby-sitter, her world turned upside down. Her questions last night had shocked Ellen, but this morning Natti had asked about the other car. Why hadn't they seen Kevin? What color was the car?

"Black," Ellen had said. She could not recall whether she had mentioned a color before. "I couldn't really tell. It was getting dark. You can't see colors in the dark."

She could not even think about that conversation without feeling sick. She was not sure exactly where the sickness came from. Probably from fear. Fear of being found out. And maybe guilt. Everything was mixed up, but the fear pounded at her relentlessly.

Natti, last night. He could have heard. Luckily he didn't. And now that she had convinced Natti of the other car, the secret was safe.

But that wasn't enough, keeping it a secret. She had to talk to someone. It was too much to handle by herself.

Mom would help her keep it straight. It already looked odd, the way she had changed her story. A delivery truck, she had said in the beginning. But the police had asked *what* delivery truck? What had just been delivered?

47

She hadn't thought of that. And because she couldn't answer, she had changed it. She made the change sound plausible enough so that no one paid much attention. But later, when they thought about it—

It *was* an accident. And if the little fiend hadn't been in the driveway— She had warned him. Hadn't she?

Oh, Kevin, I'm sorry, Kevin.

She was fond of her nephew. Only frightened. What if he died?

She was afraid of Diane. Even more than Diane, she was afraid of Mike.

"Mom?" Her voice emerged small and childish. "Mom, I can't— What if she finds out?"

"Finds out what?" Marian Hastings asked impatiently. Not impatient with Ellen, or anyone in particular, but only because of this waiting, this uncertainty. Kevin was in intensive care. They could see him for only five minutes every two hours, and he had still not regained consciousness.

"It wasn't another car," Ellen said. Her voice had diminished still further. "It wasn't anybody turning in our driveway, it was my car. He was in back of me, it was getting dark, I just didn't see—"

Marian sat a little more hunched, a little smaller-looking, and pondered this information.

Ellen's car.

"What should I do?" Ellen asked.

She waited for an answer. The answers were always there. When none came, she said again, "Mom, I don't know what to do."

"I don't know what you can do," Marian replied. "Maybe it's best just to keep it the way it is. What good will it do if you tell people what you just told me?"

"You mean, not say anything? To anybody?"

"I don't see what purpose it would serve. Do you?"

"Oh, Mom, thank you." Ellen turned to give her mother a hug. Startled, Marian found herself unable to relax and respond. Her body stiffened. In her ear Ellen sighed with relief.

"I didn't mean to do it," Ellen went on. "I just—"

"Of course you didn't mean to. But I don't understand how it happened."

"I didn't *see* him. I told you, it was getting dark and he must have been right behind the car."

"But I don't understand," Marian said again, "why you didn't check on where they were before you started backing."

Ellen dropped her hands into her lap. She mumbled, "Oh, you know," and sat staring at the floor.

Marian looked at her watch. "I think we can go in now."

Ellen followed her, dreading. The endless trouble she was in, all because of him. He should have been more careful. Even a three-year-old ought to know enough to watch out for cars. Diane should have taught him.

He was still unconscious. Looking down at him, at his blanched face that seemed thinner, somehow, and the plastic tubes for oxygen and intravenous feeding, she thought he looked dead. But he was breathing. She could see the white blanket move up and down on his chest.

Did his life hang on those support systems? she wondered. The feeding tube and the oxygen? Her eyes traveled up the oxygen tube to see where it was attached. It went directly into the wall. Marian was stroking the child's forehead and murmuring to him. "Kevin, honey, it's Grandma and Auntie Ellen. Kevin, open your eyes. Will you do that for Grandma? Just open your eyes."

49

He might wake up, Ellen thought. *He'll be the only other person who knows, and Mom wouldn't tell.*

What if Mike found out what she had done to Diane's child?

Diane saw the houses, the buildings, now far below them, like toys. A child's toy village. The trees were gray fuzz on the hillsides. She wondered how high up they were. She didn't want to ask. They would think she was afraid.

When she looked at the ground, they scarcely appeared to be moving. She was surprised that they could travel so fast and not seem to move. But they were making progress. She could see the Hudson River now. Travis banked the plane, making it feel even more precarious. Again she closed her eyes until they leveled off.

Three hours. She wondered if anyone of them would be there at the hospital. Ellen, or her mother or father. Or Mike.

That would be the hardest part, after Kevin. Seeing Mike again. It was always hard seeing Mike again, even after four and a half years. Even though she had long since stopped caring about him. It still hurt.

Travis sat with a chart on his lap, folded to show the section in which they were flying. Every now and then he and Shelley exchanged a few words, but Diane could not hear them over the roar of the engine.

Now that they had reached the river, they flew north along it. It would take them all the way to Albany. She saw a sprawl of buildings and smoke on its eastern shore and did not know whether it was Yonkers or still part of New York City.

Travis reached between the two front seats for his zippered portfolio, which he handed back to her. "There's another New York chart in there," he shouted above the engine noise. "I marked that one, too. Remember, at Albany we leave the river, and that's where the navigating gets more complicated. Why don't you study the thing and familiarize yourself with the landmarks from Albany to Massena?"

Shelley looked back at her. Diane could sense the resentment.

She found the chart and opened it, searching for Albany.

"Okay, I've got it, but what are all these purple circles around Albany?"

"Terminal control area. That's my problem, not yours. I want you to follow the line I drew to Massena. Study all the landmarks, the rivers, lakes, mountain peaks. Anything we can see from the air. You'll notice they've even marked 'cabins,' so look for clumps of cabins." He passed the chart on his lap to his daughter and told her the same thing. Good, Diane thought. Now we'll be vying with each other for the most landmarks.

She leaned forward. "The first thing is Great Sacandaga Lake. It has an arm that reaches northeast." She pointed to the chart in Shelley's hand. Shelley held it out to him, and he studied it briefly, noting the configuration of the portion of lake he was to fly over.

"Gotcha," he said, and nodded toward the river below them. "Bridge down there."

The Tappan Zee. They were barely out of the city.

"Will you know when we get to Albany?" she asked.

"I'll know. I've done all this part before, going to Plattsburgh. Except to Plattsburgh I can follow the Hudson and then Lake Champlain pretty much all the way. Makes it easy."

She imagined it would. That was what he had meant to do on this trip with Shelley. Just the two of them, and no problems. If they became lost over the Adirondacks, it would be her fault.

But it was for Kevin.

When she thought of Kevin, her mind filled with a kind of blackness. Like a tunnel at the end of the light. She wondered if it meant anything. She had never in her life had a real premonition.

Arnold Dearborn, who had been gazing glassily out of the window, reached over and took the chart from her lap. "Can I look at this a minute?"

He did not wait for an answer. The chart was folded to show the Adirondack section. She was surprised he was even interested, he seemed so preoccupied with thoughts of his wife.

She wished she had put through a second call to the hospital. Something might have changed in that hour or so. Now she wouldn't know until she reached Holland Mills.

There were three possibilities. He could be awake by now, he could still be unconscious, or he could be dead. What if she got there and learned he was dead? She shuddered to think of the telephone ringing in her empty apartment.

The plane gave a lurch. "What's that?" she asked in alarm.

"Just a little headwind," Travis replied.

Shelley had heard the apprehension in her voice and was regarding her with a faint, superior smile.

Diane managed to calm herself. "Is it going to slow us down?"

"Depends."

Headwinds. They weren't so dangerous. Maybe. She

52

had heard of planes hitting air pockets, or being slammed to the ground by peculiar vertical winds.

Dearborn still had her map. She asked, "Are you finished with that?" He handed it to her without a word and turned back to the window.

She alternated between studying the map and watching the river. She could tell by the bridges how far they had come. The Bear Mountain Bridge. Beacon–Newburgh. Poughkeepsie. Rip Van Winkle. Catskill. Each one was a kind of milestone, marking the shortening distance between Kevin and herself. But it was still too slow. It was maddening.

And then, after a while, she saw the beginning of another sprawl. A clutter of buildings, the inevitable puffs of steam and smoke. They were approaching Albany.

She looked at her watch. They had been on the way for an hour and a half. She thought they were making good time, but it felt as though the winds were increasing.

She leaned forward again. "Is this Albany?"

"This is it. You've seen it from the air before, haven't you?"

"Only from a big plane. You can't see so much from a big plane. And we're usually landing or taking off."

"This is where you catch your connecting flight?"

She nodded yes. He picked up the microphone to speak into his radio. She caught a glimpse of a river. The Mohawk or the Hudson. She was not even sure of her direction, but she thought it was the Mohawk.

They were flying right over Albany. She would not have to land, change planes, take off again. In another hour and a half they should be there. Maybe less, for they had covered slightly more than half their journey. Except that the headwinds were stronger now.

She was trying to sort out where they were when Travis spoke again. "Schenectady radio, this is Cessna N7262 at four thousand feet, traveling north northwest, destination Massena. Request weather en route."

He listened and replaced the microphone. Shelley turned to him. "What is it?"

"Nothing bad," Diane heard him say. "Just the cold front and more winds. I'd like to get to Plattsburgh before we ice up, but the winds are slowing us down a little. There's a storm coming, too, but that's later tonight, after we're all tucked in."

"Rain or snowstorm?"

"Where we're going, honey, it'll be snow."

"Oh, wow!"

Arnold Dearborn was resting against the window, watching the ground. His body seemed tense. Probably he, too, was nervous, Diane thought as another gust of wind jolted the plane.

"Travis?" she said. "How much do you think it's going to slow us down?"

"Not much. Not even enough to warrant refueling. Schenectady's probably our last chance for that."

Scarcely reassuring. But he wouldn't take risks. It was his life, too, and his daughter's.

"About an hour and a half?" she asked.

"About that."

She watched for the first landmarks. They were still in a populated area, but soon there would be nothing but mountains and lakes. She would have to distinguish one mountain, one lake, from another. There were not even any quarries, monuments, or factories, as there were in other places on the map.

Still they barely seemed to move over the ground. How

slowly each village, each ridge passed by, and the next came into view. And that gleam over there on the left. That great, gleaming sheet of water.

She pointed past Travis's shoulder. "That might be Great Sacandaga Lake."

"Probably is," he said. "That's the beginning of the Adirondacks."

They were already flying over the humps and ridges of the Adirondack foothills. The area had become more desolate. From now on their route would take them over only a few widely spaced roads, past a few tiny communities.

The earth had an exquisite look from above. Perhaps it was the smallness of each hill, each lake and pond, the velvet appearance of the bare trees.

Shelley said, "It looks like a map of it."

Again the plane shuddered and bounced.

"Are you sure we're all right?" asked Diane.

Travis said, "I'm sure. This happens all the time. If anybody's feeling sick, we've got some barf bags in my briefcase."

"That's not what bothers me," she said, although it was beginning to. "Did you file a flight plan?"

"Of course I did. What's the matter? I told you we won't fall down."

Shelley tossed her a look of scorn, and Diane subsided, once again to read the chart that was spread on her knees. She was aware of Arnold Dearborn peering at it over her arm. As he pressed closer, she looked up at him in annoyance.

"Sorry," he muttered. "I just wanted to see where we are."

"About here." She pointed to the border of the Adirondack Forest Preserve. "You should be in Montreal well before the evening."

He grunted a response. His eyes lingered briefly on the chart, and then he withdrew to his window.

She was sorry she had been abrupt. More gently, she asked, "What exactly happened with your wife? Was she in an accident?"

"Heart," he said. "Heart attack."

"That's terrible. She must be quite young."

"Yeah. She always had some kinda trouble. She had rheumatic fever when she was a kid."

"Well, I hope she feels better soon."

A dumb thing to say. You just hope she won't die, that's all, but you can't use that word.

They were flying over the long arm of Sacandaga Lake. The noonday sunshine, pouring in through the plane's windows, made the interior quite warm. Travis turned down the heater.

Shelley was pointing out the next landmarks on her chart. A series of streams. A highway. There was not much to go on. At least he had a compass, and the day was clear, with good visibility. He would be in Plattsburgh long before dark.

"How far is it to Plattsburgh from Massena?" asked Diane.

"About half an hour flying time, plus takeoff and landing."

"That's good, then. You're almost home."

She saw his cheek crease in a smile. She could not see all of his face, but the smile was attractive.

She remembered Mike and how she had loved him. Were Mike and Ellen still happy? Little whore. She was glad she had called her that. Not that it had changed anything, but she was glad.

She looked out again at the wilderness of mountain

peaks. There was something cold about it. Terribly cold. Then she realized that the interior of the plane had cooled as they gained altitude to clear the mountains.

"There's snow!" she exclaimed. "They've had snow up here."

"Not too surprising, is it?" said Travis. "Almost the end of November."

"And co—"

She never finished her simple comment. At that moment she was roughly shoved aside as Arnold Dearborn leaned toward Travis. She stared, her mind running slowly, not quite synchronized with what was happening.

"Land the plane."

Travis half turned. "What's that?"

Dearborn repeated, "Land the plane. Now. Right down there."

"I can't," said Travis. "You're crazy, I can't land here. What are you talking about?"

He hadn't seen it. He didn't know, and it was pointed at the back of his head.

"Travis," she said, as calmly as she could. "He has a gun."

9

Travis looked back. Then quickly to the front again, gripping the wheel.

The gun quivered. The man's voice rose. "Down the plane! Down the plane!"

"I can't!" Travis repeated. "Not here. Do you want to get killed?"

"You can do it." A little less certain. "You can force land. I heard of people landing on treetops."

If they could only talk him out of it . . .

The gun moved over and pointed at Shelley. Diane saw her face with the freckles stark on her nose and cheeks. Her lips were parted, her eyes staring at the gun.

"Land the plane or your daughter gets it."

"Please," said Diane. "Please let us get to Massena, at least."

"Do you hear me, mister?" The fingers settled tighter on the trigger.

If they crashed, he would be killed, too. She wanted to tell him. But the gun was pointed at Shelley. And Shelley continued to stare. Frozen.

Do as he says.

Diane could see past him through the window. Expanses of bedrock. There must be someplace to land.

She could see because Travis was circling. This time she

hadn't noticed when he banked. She felt the plane deceler-
ate.

Shoot me. Shoot me. She did not want to die on those
rocks, impaled on the trees. But she couldn't speak. And
the gun continued to point at Shelley.

They were sinking lower. Circling. She could see the
trees, the stones, larger and closer. She could see a fissure
in the rock. Branches of trees.

My God, they were going down. They brushed right
over the tops of the trees.

Down. And so fast. They would be killed. *I'm going to
die,* she thought, and wondered why she felt detached.
Watching herself die.

The plane bounced in turbulence. She heard Shelley
whimper. Without thinking, she reached out her hand and
gently placed it over the hand on the gun.

"Everybody," Travis called over the roar, "we're going to
make a forced landing. It'll be rough. Hang on."

They would fly right into the trees. They would be
shredded.

A lake! They could land on the lake. It shimmered cold
and blue in the sunshine, rippling. And then they were
over it.

A hillside rose ahead of them, bare with loose boulders.
Travis pulled back on the control wheel, and they skimmed
up over it. She heard him curse.

He banked to the left. Far away—a fire tower. Had they
seen? Maybe no one was there. No one to see a plane in
trouble.

Another stretch of bare rock, dotted with trees. He
banked again, circling. "Hang on!"

So close! My God, she could see every stone and crevice.
She hunched over, burying her face in her arms.

Travis shouted again. His voice was drowned in a metallic shriek that went on and on. The plane jolted over rocks and through trees. Her body rose and bumped back to the seat.

She heard voices. She felt someone close to her and then felt the wind on her face. She heard a man's voice saying, "They're dead."

They were dead. Travis and his daughter. Gone.

She was roused again by a loud explosion. Then all she could hear was wind in the pine trees. And she felt the cold even through her goose-down jacket. She felt it on her head and hands.

I should have worn gloves, she thought.

But it didn't matter now.

10

Shelley wasn't wearing her seat belt. Several times her father had told her to buckle up because of the turbulence, but she could see better to help him if she wasn't tied down.

At the last minute, he shouted to her. Then she remembered. She fumbled at it. Too late. She flung herself to the floor.

She was battered and bashed. Deafened by unearthly shrieks. She knew she would die.

Then it stopped. She waited for the crash. After a moment she realized they had already crashed. She took a painful breath and then another. She could breathe and she could sit up. She did not seem to be so badly hurt.

The windshield above her was broken. Her father lay slumped in his seat against the crushed door. Blood was on his face.

"Daddy?" she said.

He didn't move, but something stirred in the back seat. The man's face looked over at her. Terrified, she glanced at his hand. She didn't see the gun.

"You okay?" he asked.

She tried to remember who he was, why he was there. She could not think past the gun.

He looked different now, she noticed. The sunglasses were gone.

"You okay?" he asked again.

"I think so."

He reached inside his coat, into his jacket pocket. She watched him suspiciously. He brought out a black case, took a pair of glasses from it and put them on. They were regular ones, not sunglasses, and they magnified his eyes, which were dark and staring.

"What are you going to do?" she asked.

He blinked behind the lenses. "I'm going to get out of here."

"What about us?"

He nodded toward her father and then to the woman in the back seat. "Them two are dead."

"How do you know?"

He reached over and touched her father. She couldn't look. He said, "No pulse." Then he climbed over to the woman's side of the back seat, pushing her body out of the way.

"Open the door," he told Shelley. "I can't get out till you get out."

She struggled with the latch on the door. It was jammed, but at last she got it opened. Unsteadily, she stepped out onto the ground. Even before she was out, he pushed her seat forward, almost catching her in it.

The ground seemed closer than before. She hadn't had to climb down, only out. The landing gear must have buckled.

It was gone. The plane sat on its belly in a growth of underbrush. All around them were tall pine trees.

The man stood beside her. She still didn't see the gun. Hadn't seen it since the crash. He had used it to get here. But why here? It was nowhere, and winter was coming.

Wind blew through the trees. She was alone. *Alone*. Except for this man. He was all she had.

But she wouldn't be here, and her father would not be dead, if the man hadn't forced them down. It was very confusing.

"We'd better get out of here," he said. "It could go any minute."

"What do you mean?"

"The plane. It's leaking gas—you can smell it. The whole thing can catch fire or blow up any minute."

"But Daddy—"

"I told you, he's dead. What do you want, get yourself killed, too?"

"We can't leave him there!"

The man was unmoved. "It's up to you, kid. I'm not going to stay and get blown up."

She noticed that he had his duffel bag with him. Her own luggage was in the back of the plane, but there was no time to get it. Now she, too, could smell the fuel. She wondered how it could ignite when there was no flame. Maybe something was smoldering somewhere.

Another sharp gust of wind. They were a million miles from anywhere. She would have to go with him.

But her father. She couldn't leave her father. Only minutes ago he had been alive, talking to her, flying a plane.

Daddy, I love you.

"Okay, kid. Stay and burn up. It'll probably set the trees on fire, burn the whole place."

She couldn't think. Too much had happened, and all too fast. She couldn't believe her father was dead.

The man stood watching her. In a minute he would turn and disappear into the forest, leaving her alone.

"Are you sure he's dead?" she asked.

"Kid, get smart."

And then she saw the gun. In his hand. He was pointing it at her.

63

"You can stay if you want to," he said, "but you won't be alive."

She started at the gun, as something folded inside her. He really would kill her. Maybe he had killed her father, too. She tried to remember. She only knew he couldn't leave any of them alive. No one who had seen what happened.

"But why—"

He jerked his head, showing her the way. "It's me or the gun," he said. "Your choice. You come along and help me, or you don't."

Help him—do what? Whatever he was doing, obviously. And just as obviously, cooperating with him would be her only way of staying alive.

She started toward him. The wind whined through the trees. She looked back once more at the plane, her father's coffin. Its nose was smashed, the propeller dangling crookedly. The right wing was bent, the left one shorn off.

"They'll look for us," she said. "He filed a flight plan."

"They'll look for the plane," he told her. "Not us."

That was why he didn't want to be near the plane. Not because of fire. Her father had told her that in the event of a crash, it was always better to stay with the plane. A wrecked plane was much more visible than a person. There was a chance that searchers might find the plane, but they would never know what happened to this man. Or to her. She wondered if there was any way she could leave a mark, at least showing the direction she had taken.

But he was watching her. He had outguessed her. He waited until she was beside him and then he turned and started walking.

Stealthily, she looked back, trying to get the lay of the land. She remembered seeing a bare rocky place, where probably her father had aimed, but the plane had gone on into the trees.

He stopped suddenly. "Hey, you wait here. I forgot something. You wait, understand?"

She wanted to move, but she couldn't. If she tried to run, she would get lost. Or he would shoot her. She remained paralyzed.

From the plane came a sound like a gunshot. Her mind worked slowly. Before she could imagine what he had done, he came crashing back through the trees.

She began to shiver violently. Through chattering teeth, she asked, "Where are you going to go? You can't just stay in the woods. It's almost winter."

He looked at her with something of a smirk. "That goes for the both of us, don't it?"

If he was going to stay hidden, why did he need her? Maybe he had another plan. A person like him would have several ideas all worked out, depending on what happened.

He pushed her ahead of him. She did not see a path. She could only guess where he wanted her to go. Under the pine trees where the ground was padded with needles, there was little undergrowth. But soon they came to an area of thick bushes that scratched her hands and snapped back in her face. Roots, rocks, and weeds tripped her as she walked.

And it was cold, so cold. She was wearing a heavy jacket, but it was polyester fill, not goose down, and the wind blew through it. It blew through her jeans and through her hair, freezing her ears. She remembered the hood on her jacket and pulled it up. She had had gloves, but had taken them off in the plane so she could handle the map. She hadn't thought to put them on. Hadn't known this was going to happen.

She heard a thump and a muttered curse and looked back. He had tripped on a tree root and was stumbling, but caught himself. She would have to be alert. Maybe he would drop the gun. She couldn't see it now. It might be back in his pocket.

If he dropped the gun—what then? She would not know how to fire it. And if she did shoot him, where would she go?

Where was she going now? They were walking down a gulley. It made a sort of path, but a very rough one. She stepped on a jagged rock and turned her ankle. When she stopped to massage it, he barked, "Keep moving."

Her feet and legs ached with fatigue. The ground was too rough for walking. Dead leaves, dead vines, and stones. After a while it became a blur. She didn't think about it. Didn't think of anything, even to wonder where they were going.

She remembered this area on the chart. There had been no roads, no trace of human habitation. Not even a river to follow. Only a vast expanse of altitude.

11

Diane opened her eyes. It was cold, so cold, all around her. She looked up at the bent ceiling of some kind of vehicle. A car. She had been in a car crash, but had no idea how she had gotten there.

Then she began to remember. The plane, and Travis.

And Kevin.

My God, yes. She had been on her way to Kevin, and the plane had come down. There had been a man with a gun.

She pulled herself upright. Travis was slumped in the front seat. He looked as if he was dead. The other two were gone. Half the windshield was smashed away, leaving no protection from the cold.

"Travis."

He was resting against the door. She reached over and touched him. She saw a smear of blood on his face, and her fingers came away from his jacket stained with red.

"Travis?"

The door on her side was open. Cold. The front seat was pushed forward. They must have gotten out, Travis's daughter and the man. They must have gone for help.

She crawled toward the door and stumbled out onto the ground. She still felt groggy, but she could move.

She looked in at Travis. He might be dead. She did not

want to know. But she righted the back of the front seat and climbed in beside him.

He couldn't be. *No, no, no.* He couldn't leave her.

And the others? They must have headed for the fire tower. What if nobody was there?

She touched his arm. "Travis, please?"

He groaned. Thank God. For her own sake, she didn't care how badly he might be hurt, as long as he was there.

"Travis, wake up. We have to—" *Do what?* "We can't stay here."

He muttered something. She couldn't hear what he said.

"Wake up, Travis. We have to get out of here."

His head rolled back. He hadn't worn any covering on it. She knew a lot of body heat could be lost through the top of the head. At least she had a hood on her parka. She pulled it up over her hair.

His eyes opened. She could not tell whether he saw anything.

"T'sat . . . smell?" he asked.

"What?"

"What's . . . that . . . smell?"

She sniffed. She had not been thinking of smells. "Fuel? Is it fuel?"

"Jesus." He tried to move and clutched at his chest. She helped him to sit upright. Then he raised his left arm, slowly, grimacing, helping with the right. He wore a watch on his left wrist. A digital watch. The face was dark, the display gone.

"What time?"

She looked at her own. "A quarter—" She listened for a tick, shook it, and heard nothing.

"Great," he said.

"Why do you want to know?"

"We been here long? The fuel."

"Oh, I don't know."

"Where's Shelley?" He nodded his head as though to clear it.

"I don't know. They're gone. They must have gone for help. The door was open, and the seat was pushed forward."

"Gone for help? Here?"

"Well, it's— I don't know where they went. I blacked out, too. I heard their voices. I heard somebody talking about being dead."

"Who?"

"A man's voice. He said, 'They're dead.'"

Travis turned and regarded the open door. "Shit," he said.

"He had a gun," Diane remembered.

"Yeah."

"I don't think he'd hurt her."

"No?"

"Well, if he was going to shoot her, he'd have done it right here, and I didn't—"

"Shoot her?"

"Well—but I don't know. We just don't know."

"She's only twelve years old."

"I know that, but—" She did not know what to say. "As long as she's alive— It could be, if he was doing something illegal, maybe he wanted a hostage."

Travis seemed to consider that. "Maybe." Then he said, "Diane, there's a fuel leak somewhere. I wish I knew how long—" He tried to move. His lips drew back in pain. The instrument panel was crumpled, and he was wedged in.

"Easy," he said as she reached for him. "I think— something's broken."

He sank back, sweating and gasping. "Pretty good," he told her as he began to shake, "sweating in all this cold. Get on out of here, Di. Somebody's got to—get out of here."

"What about you?"

"Got a choice. I'll either burn or freeze to death."

"Don't talk like that, Travis, come on." She reached again. "If it were going to burn, wouldn't it have started?"

"That's why I want to know how— *No*, I can't move. Get out of here, will you?"

"You're not going to die and leave me alone. Try sucking in your breath. Come on, pull it in."

"Hurts."

"It hurts to burn alive, too. Here, I'll push and see if it does any good."

With one hand pressing on the instrument panel and the other on the seat, she tried to widen the space while Travis struggled against the pain to free himself. Every few seconds he would stop and gasp for breath. He grimaced, he cursed, but finally he was out of the narrow space. He took a moment to recover himself while Diane climbed out of the plane. Then he swung his legs through the door and tried to stand up. Instead, his knees buckled and he fell to the ground.

"Jesus Christ!" he gasped, clutching at his chest. She started toward him, but he waved her away. He picked up a handful of pine needles and sifted them through his fingers.

"Spongy ground," he commented. "Could have been worse." Then he gazed up at the trees all around them.

"Look at that. Big, beautiful evergreens."

"They are nice, but, Travis—"

"Couldn't have done a better job of hiding the plane if I'd wanted to."

"We knocked some of them down," she pointed out.

He scoffed at her optimism. "Picture yourself flying over this area. Do you think you'd notice our plane?"

"No, but—"

"I tried to land on the rocks. Couldn't stop in time."

She bent down to help him. She almost had to lift him up. His left foot seemed useless.

"Oh, boy," he said, clinging to her arm. "I think I've got a broken ankle."

"Maybe it's only sprained. Try standing on it again. If you can't, it's broken."

He lowered his foot, testing the weight.

"Hurts," he said.

"But can you stand?"

"I guess so."

"Maybe we should bandage it."

"With what? We'll need all our clothes to keep warm."

"Don't you have a first-aid kit?"

"Uh—no. I—I wasn't prepared."

"Well, how did you know we'd get forced down?"

"I didn't, but I knew we were flying over the mountains. Anything can happen. What the f—"

He reached up to his chest. His hand touched oozing blood. She noticed a darker stain on the brown of his jacket.

"There's a ho—" she began. "Did that gun go off? But this is in *front*."

"Maybe," he said, "when we crashed."

"He still couldn't—"

She remembered hearing a sound like a gunshot but could not recall when it was. "Let me see it. I don't think it's bleeding too badly, but it might get worse."

"It won't get worse." He sounded irritable. At her? Or maybe at himself.

"What do we do now?" she asked. "You can't walk very far with that ankle."

"We shouldn't walk at all. They'll be looking for the

71

plane, and we'd better be near it. Hell, I wish I knew about Shelley. I wish I knew what the hell direction they went."

"I'll see if I can find anything." She scoured the area, trying to find marks, footprints, anything. If only she could find Shelley. If she could do that for him—

Footprints in a bed of pine needles were an impossibility, she discovered, but there was one place where the needles seemed to be disturbed. Scuffed up. Maybe it meant something. But she couldn't find any more than that.

She returned to the plane to find Travis hobbling back through the path it had cut when it crashed. Out toward the rock where he had tried to land.

"Travis, what are you doing?"

"Got to set a fire," he said, "before it gets dark and colder. Got to make a camp."

"Why? We can't stay here!"

"Diane." Exasperated. "How are we going to *not* stay here? This is where we are, like it or not."

"I don't like it. How long does it take them to start looking for us?"

"Could take a day or so before they decide we're missing and get a search going. We have an electronic locator beacon on the plane, assuming it's working, but it won't do any good unless an aircraft flies over. By tomorrow it'll probably be dead."

And so, she thought, will we.

"Tell me what to do," she said.

"Shelter. And fire."

"Can't we take shelter in the plane?"

"We need a fire. There's bedrock out there. This is going to be pretty grim, Diane. All I have is a flashlight, some matches, and a space blanket."

"Well, we can—" We can what? She was so eager to do

72

something, to make up for everything, and he was so angry, and they were both doomed.

"There are a few things we can do, and we'll do them,"
he said. "If it's not enough . . ."

The clearing of bedrock was about forty feet from the
plane. Most of it was level, but one side began sloping
down the mountain. From it they could see miles of valley
and rolling ridges. They could see glimpses of a long, shining lake.

Travis stood surveying the vast, empty panorama.

"The guy must have known what he was doing," he said,
"or had a plan of some kind. He knew where he wanted to
land. Going off like that— But, God, Shelley! Oh, my
God!"

Hesitantly she put her arm around him. "Travis, I'll try
to look for her."

"No!" He pulled away. "It's useless, and you'd only
freeze to death. We've got to save ourselves, try to get
rescued, and put the authorities on it. It's the only way."

He spoke with bitterness, but he was right. They would
not be helping Shelley if they went off half-cocked and died
of exposure.

"Diane, can you help me into the plane? I'm going to try
the radio."

She supported him while he eased his way into the
damaged front seat. She wondered if the radio would even
work. The whole front of the plane was wrecked.

She heard the battery begin its rising wail. Her heart
lifted with it. He picked up the microphone.

"Mayday! Mayday! Can you read me? Anyone? This is
Cessna N7262. I'm down in the—" He glanced at Diane.
"I'm in the southeastern Adirondacks. Come in, please.
Anyone!"

He waited and then called again. It didn't really matter

that he could not give his location, because no one answered. No one heard him. They were out of radio contact with the whole rest of the world.

He switched off the power and slid back outside. "So much for that."

"We can try again later."

"Yeah. Okay, let's see what we can do about a shelter. Doesn't seem to be much around except pine, but there's plenty of that."

There was plenty, but the trees were tall and most of the branches with good needle growth were too high to reach. With Travis limping in agony, scarcely able to raise his arms, they managed to break off a number of branches, tearing their hands in the process.

Travis worked slowly. Bending and lifting made his chest feel on fire. Despite his efforts to appear normal, she could not help noticing his drained face and sweating forehead.

"Travis, you'd better take it easy. You could rip yourself apart."

"Can't afford to," he wheezed. "We don't have much time. The sun sets early."

They both looked up at the sun and found the whole sky covered with haze. Pale light still filtered through it. They had not noticed the cloudiness forming.

"Son of a bitch," he said. "They predicted a storm tonight."

Now she remembered. "Oh, Travis."

"Diane, I think we've had it, but let's keep trying."

For Kevin. And Shelley, if she was alive. Kevin had no one else. No one but her family, and that was not enough.

With her superior mobility, she continued to gather branches while he put together a crude lean-to, a low cavelike structure, which he hoped would not blow over. It was open at one side and tall enough to sit in but not stand in. It was long enough to shield them both as they lay down.

That was the only good thing that had happened to them. They had each other for moral support and body warmth. She did not want to think what it would have been like if he had been killed after all.

He used the branches with the thickest needles to line the top of the shelter. She could not see that it would keep out any cold, but it might block some of the wind. She did not really believe they would survive the night.

They gathered more branches, twigs, and needles and laid a camp fire next to their shelter. They looked for bigger pieces, logs that would burn longer, but all they could find were fallen trees. They had nothing to cut them with except Travis's knife.

When the fire was laid, he said, "I'll try the radio again." There was a flat, hopeless note in his voice. She helped him back into the plane and then went searching for logs. She found a fallen tree so decayed that she could stamp it into sections. It was mostly sawdust, but she carried the pieces back to their camp. They were slightly damp and might burn slowly enough to give a little respite from tending the fire.

"Anything?" she asked as he shuffled toward her from the plane.

"Nothing. But depending on what time it is, they ought to start figuring us missing pretty soon. Then probably tomorrow morning they'll start the search."

Tomorrow morning. If they found the plane, they would find two frozen corpses under a shelter of pine boughs.

"We don't have any food," she said. Although it didn't seem to matter. The only thing she needed was warmth.

75

"No," he agreed.

"Or water. That's more important than food. Maybe I could get to that lake down there."

"Don't be crazy, Diane, that's miles away. And what would you carry water in?"

She was grasping at straws. The water was hypothetical anyway. They would not live long enough to become dehydrated.

"Signal fire," he said.

She nodded. They had already built a fire, but okay. At least the exertion had a warming effect.

"We'll put it on the far side of this rock," he told her, "because it's going to smell like hell on wheels."

"Why? What are you planning to burn?"

"Rubber tires. Stuff like that. We need black smoke. Forest fires are usually white. If it's black—and anybody sees it—they'll know it has to do with airplane wreckage."

"That's the catch, then," she said. "Somebody has to see it."

"Well, yes."

"And do you think somebody will, besides an owl or a hawk?"

"They will start searching for us, Di. But let's do it now, in case something comes over. Who knows, we might be somewhere near the New York–Montreal air route."

"If we are, it's awfully quiet."

"Yeah."

"I'm sorry, Travis. I'm not being fair. You're doing an awfully good job of keeping your spirits up, and you're hurt, too. At least I'm not hurt."

"It's just that I think we have a chance."

She did not see how he could really think so.

"Rubber tires," she said. "I saw one of the wheels in those bushes there."

76

With his knife he carved chunks from the tire. He cut out large hollow pieces that he filled with oil drained from the crankcase.

She searched the forest and found the rest of the landing gear, which had been torn off when they hit the ground. Even that process, she supposed, had helped to cushion their landing. The wheels and wings, as they were shorn away, had taken most of the shock. It might have saved their lives. But for what?

They added pine branches and dried needles to make it blaze quickly when an aircraft was spotted. Diane went out to the middle of the bedrock and again scanned the sky. It was entirely clouded over now. The sun was only a bright spot in the clouds.

So that was the southwest, over there where the sun was. And Massena was north-northwest. Where Kevin was.

She hoped the clouds were high enough so that a search plane could fly below them.

12

Shelley clutched at her side. It felt as though she had been stabbed with a giant carving knife. She was sure her feet were swollen inside her running shoes, but still she stumbled on. When they studied World War II in school, she had read about forced marches and had wondered how anybody could drop dead just from walking, but now she understood. At any moment she might fall. If she did, she would not be able to get up. She would welcome death.

She turned her head and saw that he still had the gun in his hand. It was pointed at the ground.

"How much farther?" she asked.

"Just keep moving." Probably he didn't even know where he was going.

For a while he had walked in front of her, leading the way. She had followed because she did not want to be left alone in the forest. Then they came to something that resembled a path, and he had sent her in front again.

If it was a path, she thought, there might be people around. Unless it was a deer trail.

Or, if there were people, they were probably around only in summer.

The sky had clouded, and it was even colder now. Soon it would be night. By now she was supposed to have been in her grandparents' warm house. She wondered how long it would be before they worried enough to call her mother. Before any of them worried enough to report the plane missing.

Even then, no one would know where to find her.

Through the trees she caught a glimpse of something white. At first she thought it was the sky and that she was on the edge of a cliff, looking out. Then she saw it again and realized it was a lake reflecting the white, cloudy sky.

The path turned more steeply downward. It became rougher, rockier. On the steepest parts, she had to grab branches and saplings to keep from slipping.

Finally, after countless twists and turns, the path reached the edge of the lake. The entire shore was encrusted with ice for several yards out. They walked just inside the ring of ice, on the rocks along the shore, rocks so rounded and lumpy that it was impossible to gain much footing.

I'll die, she thought. If she ran out to the edge of the ice, perhaps she could drown herself. She had to walk along not thinking about her feet at all.

After a while she looked up and, in the distance, saw a house. An isolated cabin. For an instant she felt she had known it was there. Then she realized that *he* had known it was there and had it all planned. Or at least he knew there would be something like it on a lake shore in the mountains.

Soon they picked up a path that ran along the lake's edge. It was still rocky, and she had to watch where she was going. From time to time she would raise her eyes and see the house. It was not a mirage. She felt reassured. But it was far away. She blotted time and distance from her mind.

Until they were almost there. It was shelter. Shelter at last. A crude brown-stained, box-shaped cabin.

The door was fastened with a padlock. He made her stand back while he shot it off. She heard the shot echoing against the rocks across the lake.

He made her go in ahead of him. Her feet and hands were frozen, and she was ready to go inside, even with him.

The cabin was as cold as the outdoors. She was out of the wind, but the dankness and mustiness made a seeping, bone-chilling cold. She felt as though it would go on forever. She would never be warm again.

It was a one-room cabin with two wooden bunks built into one corner. In the center of the floor was a wood-burning stove, ice cold. Wooden shelves ran along two walls.

He looked over the shelves, taking an inventory of the food supplies. There was not much. Half a jar of A & P instant coffee. Two cans of peaches and one of creamed corn. The remnants of a five-pound bag of Domino sugar, spilling out through a hole that had probably been gnawed by mice. There were mouse droppings everywhere, on the shelves, on the cold top of the stove, on the sleeping bag that covered the lower of the two bunks.

"Huh!" he said in disgust.

She tried to quiet her chattering teeth. She felt bolder now, not really caring whether she lived or died. Probably he would kill her anyway. "What did you expect?" she asked. "After all, you're trespassing, aren't you?"

His eyes passed over her, not connecting with what she said, and unconcerned.

On a corner shelf, half buried under a dirty piece of cloth, he found a small propane stove. He took it out, investigated, and discovered that the cylinder was empty. "Huh!" he said again. This time she shared his disappointment. She wanted warmth, any kind of warmth. Even a single flame.

"You could cook on the wood-burning stove," she said. "There's nothing to cook, anyway."

"You cold?" he asked.

"I'm dead." She huddled deeper inside her jacket, a shivering ball.

"We gotta get some wood."

It meant going back into the wind. But wood was all around them. In a few minutes they had gathered enough to start the fire. He took a small hatchet from his duffel bag and cut their collection of fallen limbs and branches to fit the stove.

He had also, she noticed, brought several disposable cigarette lighters. A down sleeping bag and a down parka. Thermal underwear, chukka boots, and other warm clothing. A large pack of dried rations. He was entirely prepared for survival in the wilderness. Perhaps for a long time.

"What are you running away from?" she asked.

"Who says I'm running away?" He lit a cigarette lighter and held it inside the stove. Its flame caught on dry leaves and soon flared up, casting an amber glow onto his face.

"I, uh—" She did not want to make him angry.

He fanned the flame ineffectually with his hand. The fire danced and crackled inside the stove.

He said, "You want to know, kid? You might as well know."

He was so deadpan, she couldn't tell whether he was being belligerent, sarcastic, or sincere. "Not if you don't want to talk about it," she managed to say.

"You might as well know. You and I aren't going to have no secrets from each other. So you can get over that fancy idea. No separate bedrooms."

She knew he was leering, but she would not look at him. If she could avoid his eyes . . .

"I blew away some cops," he said.

"You what?"

"I blew away a couple a cops."

She stared at him. The words were almost meaningless. Because it didn't mean anything to *him*.

"That ain't what started it," he went on. "It was armed robbery. That's the name they give it. Plus possession of a weapon and felony murder. So it ain't healthy when the cops start poking around. It ain't healthy for the cops, either. You understand, kid?"

She didn't believe him. He was probably bluffing. Trying to sound big.

She asked, "What's felony murder?"

"Homicide during the commission of a felony."

She didn't believe that, either. Except that he did have a gun. And he had threatened to use it.

"What's a felony?"

"A crime. Okay? They call it a crime. Armed robbery. If you kill somebody during an armed robbery, that's a felony murder."

Gradually she began to understand.

"Who— Who—"

"A kid, okay? A kid just like you. It was her fault. I told 'em not to move."

The understanding faded. It couldn't have been a kid. You don't hold up a kid with a gun. He was only trying to frighten her.

"What are you planning to do?" she asked. "You can't stay here forever."

He prodded the fire with a stick and closed the stove. "Long enough," he said.

82

"Well, what did you bring me for? Won't I get in the way?"

"I brought you," he said, "because you wanted to come."

She gasped. "But I—"

"You didn't want me to leave you up there with them two."

She felt angry and afraid at the same time. That was not how it had been. He had threatened her with the gun.

"You said you'd kill me."

"I said that? You think back, kid. Did I say that?"

"You said, if I stayed there, I wouldn't be alive."

"You wouldn't be. Do you hear that wind? You'd be freezing to death up there with them two dead bodies."

Was that what he had meant? She didn't think so, but it might have been. Then maybe he was not as ruthless as she had thought. After all, he had brought her to this cabin and lit the fire.

She didn't know. She didn't know anything except that she was a prisoner. And that she needed him to help her stay alive.

It was growing dark inside the cabin. He investigated a hurricane lantern, but found no fuel for it. Their only light was the glow from the stove.

Timidly, she asked, "Can you help me get back to my mother?"

He snickered. "No way. We're not going nowhere, kid. Only if you get your story straight about what happened up there, then maybe I can trust you."

"I won't tell anybody about you."

"You're damn right you won't."

She felt a rising panic. She fought it down and said, "You'd be safer and better off alone, without me eating half the food."

83

"You won't eat half the food," he assured her.

She would starve. But he couldn't have meant to stay here all winter.

She watched him squatting before the fire, the orange light glinting on his glasses. She was only beginning to feel its warmth and wanted to go over and stand next to it, but he was there.

She wandered over to the bunks. Probably he would make her take the upper one, but it was only a bare board. There was no mattress and no cover.

A ladder led up to it. She could climb up there now, but—she looked back at him—it might be inviting trouble. Instead she sat on a wooden folding chair near the window. She could feel a gale blowing in around the frame, and it froze her, but she was not near him.

She closed her eyes, exhausted. It was too cold by the window to sleep and too uncomfortable in the chair. She heard him walking toward her.

"Who do you know in Massena?" he asked.

She opened her eyes, aware that he had startled her into looking guilty.

"Nobody."

"Don't give me that. What were you going there for? Turkey day?"

"Only to take that woman. My father's friend. Her kid's in a hospital there. Then we were going to Plattsburgh where my grandparents live."

"Your grandparents know you were coming?"

"Of course they do."

She wondered if her father had notified them that they were coming a day early.

But there were other factors at work. She knew why the man was asking. She said, "My dad filed a flight plan."

"Yeah? So what?"

"That means if we don't show up in Massena by this afternoon, they'll start looking for us."

"Yeah? What'll they find?"

A wrecked plane with two bodies. Her father—dead.

She clenched her teeth. If she ever gave way— If she ever let it be real—

13

Jerry Mercer glanced at his watch. The broad was taking forever just to look through a few mug shots. He had pinned high hopes on her after the confident description she had given. Now she seemed uncertain and a bit rattled.

"I don't know." She ran a silver fingernail lightly down the page. "He was sort of like both of these."

Two guys, each wearing a mustache. One had a slightly bulbous forehead and a weak jawline. The other had a chubby face and acne-marked cheeks. She was going by the mustache. Nothing else.

"Take off the whiskers," Jerry said.

Chuck Baroni, who was standing in back of the girl, looked up at him briefly, but said nothing. Chuck was in charge of the investigation. Jerry had nothing to do officially, but because it had been his own kid, they let him sit in.

"How about a sketch?" Baroni suggested.

"Listen," Jerry told the girl, "close your eyes and try to see the guy without a mustache. Did he have a long face? Round? Fat? Skinny?"

"No, he wasn't a fat man."

"I'm talking about his face."

"Gee . . ."

She couldn't remember. He was not surprised. Very few people could recall even the most obvious details.

She compared the mug shots again. "Maybe he was more like this one." The guy with the bulbous forehead. "Except for his forehead."

Jerry took out his cigarettes. He had promised Doris he'd start cutting back, but this was driving him up the wall. It looked as if there wasn't to be a real identification after all. They'd have to start with a sketch. And he'd hoped—

But she wasn't finished. Baroni put in a marker where the two mustaches were, and she turned the page.

Jerry remembered his daughter talking about this girl, Gina Wallek. Becky thought of her as an older woman, cheap but sophisticated. She was older than Becky, anyway. Gina said she was nineteen, but he doubted it. She was more like twenty-six or seven. She wore a lot of eye makeup. Must have taken her hours every day to get it all on. And those exquisitely ovaled nails. The whole bit, just for a fried-chicken shop. She ought to have been in show business. Probably she thought so, too.

With tormenting slowness, she turned another page. Her finger hovered, circling the air, and then stopped. Her lips moved as though she were talking to herself. Then she went on.

He had to remind himself that she was Becky's friend. She was doing her best. When she gave her initial description, it had all been fresher in her mind, although sometimes that was the worst time. Maybe she had been *too* willing, ready to say and believe almost anything, just to help.

"You know," she said, "in some of those fancy boutique places, they keep the door locked. They won't let anybody in without a good look at them first. Sometimes I wish I could work in a place like that."

One hell of a town, Jerry thought, where you had to keep

a store locked tight even during store hours. But it was true. He knew a lot of places like that.

Thinking of stores brought back fleeting memories of walking down Fordham Road with Doris and some of the kids when they were younger. Becky, Angie, and Rick. Saturday shopping. A hot summer day. Holding Becky's hand, buying them frozen custard. The happy times.

He never should have let her take that job. He should have moved his family out to Valley Stream, someplace like that, on the Island, where they'd have a chance. When the kids were little, he couldn't afford it. He could afford it even less now, with housing costs always a few miles ahead of him, a dream at the end of a rainbow. Always ahead of him.

Again the silver finger stopped.

"That one," she said.

Both men bent over her to see it. Baroni asked, "You sure now?"

"I'm sure. That's the shape of his face. Everything."

"Ty Hannon," said Baroni. "Armed robbery. It figures."

"Do you think you can find him?" asked the girl.

"We always try, miss. And if we do, we'll be in touch with you."

"You mean I'll have to come in and—"

"We'll find him," Jerry said. He was studying the picture. A heavy face. Other people had described him as slender. He supposed you could have a slender body and a heavy face.

The girl was putting on her coat. Jerry said, "We appreciate your help, Miss Wallek."

"You're her father, aren't you?" she asked.

"Yep. She was my oldest. She talked about you."

"She was a good kid. A real nice kid. I hope you catch this—" She nodded toward the book.

The way she looked at him, for an instant she reminded him of a rabbit. Then she got busy with her coat again, tying the belt.

Jerry drove her home. He had some time before the other witnesses could get there. Even though he wasn't official, he did not intend to miss any of it.

He wondered if she had been right about Ty Hannon. Something bothered him, but he couldn't quite figure what it was. In any case she had seemed awfully sure, and her description had been good.

After he dropped Gina at her apartment, he drove to a stationery store and bought a map of the five boroughs. Back in the car he spread it out on the seat beside him and followed the killer's trail from the Bronx to the Thirty-fourth Precinct in Manhattan. No one else thought there was any connection. They all thought he was crazy, and maybe he was, with nothing to go on but his hunch and a pair of glasses. It hadn't even been the same weapon. The two cops had been shot with a different gun, a higher caliber than the one that killed Becky.

Still, the hunch would not go away, so he had to use it.

Okay, assuming he was right, here was a guy who had killed three people, two of them cops. An experienced criminal, he would know better than to stick around and try to be invisible. Where would he go?

As far as could be determined, he was traveling alone and on foot, or by public transportation. It had been close to eleven at night. Where would he go?

God dammit, he could go just about anywhere. He could jump on a train and ride to the far end of Brooklyn. He could hop a bus, if they ran that late, and head for New Jersey. The first thing to do was check out Ty Hannon, where he lived, the people he knew.

Only thing was, if Ty Hannon had half a brain, right now

he wouldn't be where he lived or associating with the people he knew. Which left an awful lot of world where he *could* be.

When Jerry returned to headquarters, he found Chuck Baroni talking with a young Hispanic couple.

"This is Mr. and Mrs. Nuñez, Jerry. They were there in the restaurant."

"Yeah, he told me to empty my pockets," said Mr. Nuñez. Rafael, his name was. Jerry remembered seeing it on the list. His wife was Migdalia.

"You got mug shots?" Nuñez asked. He, too, seemed sure of himself. All these people, who must have been terrified out of their heads with a gun pointing at them, were awfully sure they remembered the face behind the gun.

"You wait, ma'am, okay?" Baroni said to Migdalia. She was small and wide-eyed and looked as if she might be about Becky's age. He explained, "It's better if each of you do it separately, without knowing what the other one said."

She sat down and waited outside while her husband went in to look at the pictures.

He skimmed through them quickly, not like Gina. Maybe too quickly. Maybe he wasn't really seeing them.

"His eyes," Nuñez said. "The way he looked at you. He could knock off his own grandmother, I don't know."

"What color were his eyes?" asked Baroni.

"Dark. He had on glasses, see. Dark brown, I guess."

"What kind of glasses?"

"I don't know. Round. The glass part was round. And silver—"

"Not gold?"

"No, silver, I remember. Or steel. I don't know too much about glasses."

"What about his hair?"

"Dark. Straight. He had a dark mustache."

"Was he wearing anything on his head?"

"No, nothin'."

"You sure? Nothing? No cap? Hat?"

"Nothin'. Just his hair. It wasn't too long, you know? It was short hair. Short in back."

"What about his clothes?"

Nuñez scratched his chin. "I don't know. Pants. Jeans, maybe. I don't know. He had a brown jacket. That's right. Wool, like. What's that stuff where it's different colors?"

"Tweed?" suggested Baroni.

"I guess. It was brown and some white. It looked old. Tacky-looking."

An instantaneous impression. That was the only way he could have done it. The man must have had a photographic memory.

Or an imaginative one.

They started with the book that had Ty Hannon's picture in it. Jerry waited, his mouth dry with anticipation, while Nuñez turned the pages. Finally he reached the last one.

Baroni said, "Nobody in there looked like him?"

"I didn't see nobody."

"You sure? Try and imagine his face without the glasses."

"And the mustache," added Jerry.

They opened the next book. And the next. Finally Nuñez stopped and bent down for a closer look.

"Wow!" he said.

"What wow?" asked Baroni.

Nuñez examined the picture again. "No, I don't know. The eyes look like him. I don't know. Maybe not."

"Which is it? Maybe or not?"

"I don't know. I didn't see him so good. I was— And the whole thing only took a minute."

"Right," said Baroni. It summed up, in a nutshell, a

crime witness's identification. And it was true. Under the circumstances, who could ask them to do any better? Jerry tried not to let the disappointment kill him.

Mrs. Nuñez was next. She, too, insisted that the man's glasses had been steel rimmed instead of gold.

"I remember," she said, "how cold his eyes were, like ice. And the glasses were like ice. You never saw gold ice."

"What was his face like?"

She rubbed her hands up and down on her cheeks. She did not know how to describe him. A thinnish face, Baroni elicited, when he saw that she was compressing her own face with the gesture.

"It's hard," he said to Jerry over the girl's head. "You can get a good look at a person, but you can't always put it in words." A polite way of saying they could rarely put it into words. Most people simply did not have the vocabulary or did not know how to use what they had.

The girl agreed. She seemed grateful for Baroni's understanding. It made her more eager to cooperate. With his coaching, a description gradually emerged. Not much of one, but probably all they would get. She looked through the pictures and picked out two she said bore some resemblance to the man. Neither her choice nor her husband's was Ty Hannon.

After she left, Baroni said, "Okay, here's what we've got. That's two votes for steel-rimmed glasses, one for gold. One positive for a navy blue knitted cap, one positive and one possible for a bare head. One vote for Ty Hannon, one maybe, later withdrawn, for a dude named Arlie Dean, and one nothing."

"And it probably isn't any of those," Jerry said. "All these people were under stress."

With physical pain, he felt the stress his own daughter

must have been under in those last moments. For her the dreaded horror had come true.

Chuck said, "You're bearing up well, Jerry."

"Yeah," he agreed. It helped if he kept busy. The investigation was therapeutic, and he hoped it would be fruitful. Once it was over, he would probably go bananas.

"How about some coffee?" asked Chuck.

"I'll get it," Jerry said. Another way of keeping busy. He went out for two coffees and brought them back, steaming and paper-smelling. Even in Styrofoam cups, brown-bagged coffee still smelled of cardboard. They sat at Baroni's desk and reviewed the facts about their suspect.

Ty Hannon, born in Hoboken, New Jersey. Present whereabouts unknown.

"Great," said Chuck.

Served time for a gas station robbery. Arrested as a suspect in a second gas station robbery, released on bail, disappeared.

"You want to check out the other?" Jerry asked.

"What other?"

"The one he wasn't sure about."

"He said it wasn't, remember?"

"He said maybe not. It doesn't hurt to check him out."

Jerry didn't want to lean on it. If he made a nuisance of himself and got their backs up, they wouldn't let him near the investigation.

"Arlie Dean," said Chuck. "Born in Amsterdam, New York, wherever the hell that is. Present address, Manhattan. How come New York gets all the good guys? Served time in Dannemora, escaped, recaptured after eighteen months. He was found working as a janitor in some hotel upstate."

"Where's he supposed to be now?" asked Jerry.

"I told you, Manhattan. He's on parole, so we can find him if we need him."

"You hope."

The next witness was Henry Perkins, a sixty-five-year-old black man.

"He told me to pull down my pants," Perkins sputtered. "Didn't want me to be no hero, I guess, and go chasing after him. I didn't even get my belt undone when he shot that kid."

What had the gunman worn on his head?

"Nothin', that I can remember."

Any distinguishing features?

"Yeah, glasses. I remember that. Couldn't see his eyes, 'cause the light shined on his glasses. He had a mustache, too."

"You couldn't see his eyes?"

"Well, for a minute I did, but mostly I didn't. It depended which way the light was shining."

He looked through the mug shots but couldn't find the man.

"I'd know him anywhere. That face was just plain *evil*. It was a devil's face if I ever saw one. It'd take a man like that to shoot a little girl."

"What did he have on?"

"A coat. Jacket. Speckled, like. Brown, I think."

"Anything on his head?"

"Don't remember anything."

Baroni said, "Thanks, Mr. Perkins. We'll be in touch. If we bring in any suspects, we'll ask you to come in again—"

"Sure," said Perkins cheerfully. "Be happy to. I never seen a lineup."

There was one more witness. It was Jerry's neighbor Vernon Grady, who came in later that evening. No one knew he had been at the store until he heard about the shooting and went to offer his condolences.

"I don't even know if I saw the man," Grady explained when he arrived at the station. "Somebody was coming in just as I went out. I guess it must have been him. I didn't really look at him, but I'll see what I can do."

He remembered the glasses. He thought they were steel rimmed, not gold. He remembered the mustache but not what was worn on the head. He had a vague recollection of a tannish jacket.

He looked at the mug shots but kept shaking his head. "I don't really remember. I was going out and I hardly noticed him."

He paused at several of the pictures but shook his head again.

"I dunno. See, I was going out and he was coming in, and I didn't really look at him. I just can't say for sure. I wish I could, Jer."

14

As Shelley had expected, he gave her the top bunk, probably so she could not sneak away without his knowing. He had also let her take the sleeping bag that had been on the lower bunk, not out of generosity, but because he had a good down bag of his own. A nice, clean one. She had shaken out the mouse droppings as well as she could. It still gave her the horrors to lie in it. She found herself shrinking from the flannel lining, but it was better than the sharp, numbing cold.

She lay in the dark, listening to the wind howl around the cabin, feeling it blow through cracks and chinks. At one point the man had gotten up and pressed some rags around one of the windows. In the faint glow from the stove she saw him pause and then run his finger through something on the window ledge.

"It's snowin'," he said.

That was his only comment. She wondered how deep it would snow. Would they be stuck there in the cabin? For how long?

They had eaten the can of creamed corn for dinner, and he had opened one of the peaches. She hadn't wanted any. The corn, on top of everything else that had happened, made her ill. He had munched on some of his beef jerky, not offering her any.

That left a can and a half of peaches, the coffee and the sugar. And his own dried rations.

Maybe he would hunt. He would bring in a rabbit or a deer and expect her to cook it for him, and she would be sick all over again. When he had unrolled his sleeping bag, she discovered he had a shotgun, in addition to the handgun. Was that for hunting, she wondered, or for shooting at police and park rangers?

She thought of her father up there on the mountaintop. Dead. She couldn't believe it. Truly gone. Forever and ever. And alone. Except for that woman, whoever she was. She didn't think it likely that anyone would see the plane down there among the trees, even if they searched for it. He would remain there exactly as she had left him. No one would find his body until perhaps sometime in the spring or summer. Or maybe not for years.

She heard the man breathing loudly and steadily. He was asleep. She could allow herself to cry now. She buried her face in the rough, pilled flannel of the sleeping bag and felt the tears well up in her eyes.

Huddled under their space blanket and a layer of pine boughs, in the shelter that was not really a shelter, Diane and Travis shivered so violently that sleep was impossible.

Because of the wound in his chest, Travis found he could lie only on his back. She lay tightly against him as they tried to keep each other warm. From time to time she would reach out and put another branch on the fire.

"If we ever get out of here," she said into his ear, "I'm going to spend the rest of my life in an overheated apartment, and I'm going to stay wrapped in ten blankets all the time, even in summer. And I'll make them turn off the air conditioning in my office."

"Air conditioning," Travis repeated in almost a purr. "Just think, in a few months you'll be complaining about the heat."

"Never."

"The mugginess. Remember New York in summer?"

She tried to remember how it was. To feel the sultriness, the oppressive humidity. She could feel nothing but cold.

"If you hadn't made this bed," she told him, "I think we'd have rigor mortis by now."

Travis was an experienced camper, but not a survivalist. Still, he had performed a neat trick, she thought. He had dug a trench under the shelter, large enough for them both to lie down in. He had filled it with stones heated in the camp fire and piled the loose earth and pine needles back over the stones. She could feel the warmth radiating up through their earthen mattress. She wondered how long it would last. If all night, it might take the fatal edge off the cold.

She had found Shelley's gloves on the floor of the plane. Poor Shelley. She must be wanting them badly—if she was still alive—but they were some protection to Diane's hands as she reached again to stoke the fire.

"Travis, I just felt something on my face."

"Yeah? What sort of something?"

"It felt like—snow."

"Mmm," he mumbled, half asleep. Then, with an effort, drawled, "Weather—prediction."

"Travis, don't go to sleep!"

"I think it's okay, Di. I think we're warm enough."

"If it snows—"

"It'll keep us warm."

She supposed if they went to sleep and didn't wake up, they would never know it. She was not ready yet, but what choice did they have?

He had thought the warm stones would keep them alive, but she was too cold to sleep. He thought they needed sleep for survival, but she was afraid of not waking up.

"Don't leave me, Travis."

He reached up with his right arm, then winced with the pain in his chest.

"We're okay," he said again. "I promise."

"Do you have enough matches so we can do this tomorrow night?"

"Plenty of matches. But we'd better keep the fire going all day."

They had built a windbreak of stones around the fire. Most of the wind blew from the north, onto their backs. It blew through the shelter, but at least the shelter protected them from the blowing snow and stinging particles of ice.

She thought she would have to sleep. But only for a while. She would wake herself in half an hour and put another branch on the fire.

She woke, remembering that no one knew where she was. Only Travis's ex-wife and Bill Adams at the airport, and they didn't know her name.

She hadn't told her family when she was coming. They would expect her on a commercial flight, if at all. No one would think to connect her with a small plane down in the Adirondack mountains.

It was still dark and very cold. She couldn't see the fire. She pushed herself up with her hand and looked out at the expanse of blue-white.

"Travis! Travis, the fire!"

"Huh?"

"It's gone. It's buried."

He sat up, disarranging their pine-bough quilt. "Son of a bitch," he said.

The snow reflected enough light so that they could see shadows and outlines. They could see a basin of snow where the fire had been. Snow was piled around them and still falling, blowing, drifting. Only the shelter had kept them from being half buried.

"Maybe we could make an igloo," he said without enthusiasm, "except I think you need water."

"If we light another fire, we'll have plenty of water."

"Diane, you're a genius."

She was hardly that. She had gotten them into this. He had been reluctant to take the extra passenger, and she had urged him. She had fallen for the sob story, identified with it. If not for her, Travis would be safe and warm in his parents' house.

He tried to sit up and failed. The pain seared his entire chest.

"I'll do it," she said. "I think you strained yourself too much already."

She removed the snow from their fireplace and gathered more twigs and needles. Sheltering it from the wind with her own body, she lit a new blaze.

"Lucky it wasn't rain," she said. "At least our wood is mostly dry."

He made no response. His eyes were closed. She would have to get him warm somehow.

"Tell me how to make an igloo," she said. "I'll do the work if you'll just tell me how."

Another effort. He opened his eyes and stared straight upward.

"Don't know how. I've only seen cartoons. Don't know what they really look like." He tried to reach out to her. "Come on, Diane, give it up."

"I won't give up!" His apathy alarmed her.

"Can't stand to see you kill yourself."

"You mean your *machismo* won't let you lie there while I do the work. Okay, it's not work. I just want to move around and keep myself warm."

His eyes drifted closed, and she began to pack the snow in a circle around the shelter and the fire.

Like Travis, she had no idea what a real igloo looked like. She doubted that they were constructed of the neat, rectangular bricks depicted by cartoonists. Just something that would hold together. She packed more snow, building her wall higher and higher, with a burning stick for her welding torch. It gave her a sense of satisfaction to see Travis protected as the wall grew in height. He would substitute for Kevin. Even for herself. She wouldn't let him die.

She lost all sense of time. The work helped to keep her mind from the numbing cold. Briefly she considered the fact that as long as the storm lasted no search planes would be flying overhead. Still, in a way, the snow was a blessing. It enabled her to build this shelter, which would offer more warmth and protection than the pine boughs had done. The snow would also provide them with water.

She watched the day dawn, gray and still snowing. *Rain before seven, done by eleven.* Too bad it wasn't true.

She had almost finished the igloo. The roof was the hardest part. She remembered all she had known of architecture and how a certain kind of curve could support its own weight. Her hands were numb. She never could have done it without Shelley's gloves. Where was Shelley now?

She crawled inside to find Travis awake. He blinked at her. "You did it."

"It doesn't look like much, but it might keep some of the cold out."

"You did it."

"Oh, Travis." She lay down beside him and began to cry.

She felt him trying to reach her with his good arm. She crawled on top of him, careful to guard his wound. Could it have been a bullet? If so, it must have just missed his heart.

101

"Don't, Di." He patted her helplessly. She did not know whether he was saying her name or "Don't die."

"It's still snowing," she wept.

"It'll stop."

That was true. It never snowed forever. It always stopped sometime.

"We're going to get out of this, Diane."

Her lips touched his cheek. "Travis, you feel hot."

"That's something, isn't it?"

"You've got a fever."

"Better than the other way."

Better than hypothermia. But a fever was not good, either. Probably his wound was becoming infected.

"We have to get you out of here."

"We're staying right here, Diane. We'll stay until they find us."

She did not like the way it sounded. At least to her.

Shelley woke, having to go to the bathroom. It was growing light inside the cabin. She could see snow piled up at the windows. Light was coming through the snow, but it was dim, gray light.

She wondered how she could manage it. If she climbed down the ladder, he would wake. He would probably follow her. He would watch. And there was no place to go but that freezing outdoors.

She did not want to wake him. The longer he slept, the happier she was, if she could be happy at all, but she had to go badly. She sat up, turned around, and put one foot on the ladder.

He grunted. She started down.

"Where do you think you're going?"

She stopped. "I have to pee, if you don't mind."

He scrambled out of his sleeping bag. "Not without me, you don't."

"Listen, where would I go? There must be ten feet of snow out there."

He grunted again, then put his feet on the floor. He had taken off his boots, but he wore heavy socks.

"I'm gonna be watching you," he said.

"That's not nice."

She had meant to be flip, to show she was not afraid of him. But she realized again what might happen, and it did not seem such a remote possibility. What could she do? Be ugly? Make him think she was deformed? Diseased? Then he might dump her into the snow and leave her there.

Maybe it would happen anyway, no matter what she tried. She wondered if it would hurt. She felt as though it might tear up her insides.

He sat on the edge of the bunk, not moving. Maybe he didn't mean to watch her too closely. She walked over to the door and pulled it open. A cascade of snow tumbled in. The drift outside was piled up higher than her knees. She glanced back at him. He still hadn't moved. Maybe he knew she couldn't escape. She would never be able to walk through this.

She pushed the snowdrift away from the door. Farther out, it was not as deep. But all she had on her feet were running shoes, and they quickly filled with cold snow. She fought her way around to the corner of the house and hastily urinated. She hoped he couldn't see her, but she almost didn't care. Pulling up her jeans, she hurried back inside and emptied her shoes.

"I guess you're stuck here," she told him, "unless you have snowshoes."

"Mind your own business, kid."

She felt her face change color. She had thought it was her business, since she assumed that, if he left, he would take her with him. But perhaps he didn't intend to.

"You wouldn't leave me!" she cried. Fragmentary plans flashed through her mind. What would she eat? How to keep warm? What if it snowed until the cabin was buried?

"I didn't leave you at the plane, did I?" he asked.

"No." They had talked about that yesterday. She thought he had had a gun. He said she wanted to go with him. She didn't remember. She wanted to stay with her father, but he was dead.

"I don't know."

"What do you mean you don't know?" He began pulling on his chukka boots. They were high ones that needed lacing all the way up. They would not be high enough for all the snow.

"I was scared," she said.

"Yeah? Scared to get left alone up on the mountain with them bodies? You know where you'd be right now if I left you there."

"I'd be dead."

"Damn right. So you can thank me for letting you come along."

She reflected on that for a moment. "But if it wasn't for you, I'd be in Plattsburgh right now with my grandparents. And my father would be alive."

"That right? You blaming me for the plane crash?"

"But it—it didn't—"

"Kid, come over here."

He was still sitting on the edge of the bunk, lacing his boots. Slowly she approached him. She wondered what he would do. Would he try to rape her? But he wouldn't be putting on his boots—would he?

"Bring over that chair," he said, pointing to the one next

to the window, "and sit down. We gotta get this straight."

She obeyed him, but she didn't like what he said. Get what straight?

"Look," he began, when she had sat down a few feet away from him. "You heard the engine noise yesterday."

"Yes." Of course she had heard the engine noise. You couldn't get away from it, especially in a small plane.

"You heard when it started getting funny. And then we were going down, and your dad was fighting with that wheel thing trying to get us back up."

"No! You said—"

He held up his hand. "Will you listen to me? Your dad was fighting with that wheel, but the plane was going down. Then he said we'd have to make an emergency landing. Remember that?"

She did. Her father had said that. He had said "Hang on," but she didn't have her seat belt fastened, and she flung herself to the floor.

"But you had a gun!" she exclaimed. "You told him to land."

"Who said I had a gun?"

"She— I— You had it. You had your hand on the back of the seat, and you had a gun."

"I had my hand on the back of the seat, hanging on."

"But you—"

"Listen, that woman was a little bit nervous. Maybe I had my finger pointed, hanging onto the seat. Maybe I even took out my gun, I do that sometimes when things are getting rough, it's a habit, but I put it away again. I put it in my pocket. It's there right now, you want to see it?"

She shook her head. She felt very strange, very confused. She had seen the gun, or thought she did. He had pointed it at her. He had said—

He went on, "Sure, I was saying 'You can land there.'

See, I could tell there was something wrong with the plane, and it's better to land, even hard, than wait till it crashes. You have a better chance of coming through."

Had he really said that? She wanted to believe him. She wanted it all to be a terrible, unavoidable accident, rather than anyone's fault. Especially this man, on whom she depended. She did not want him to have killed her father.

"Is that really what happened?" she asked.

"That's really what happened. Why would I lie to you? What have I got to win or lose by lying? You have your story, but who'll you tell it to, am I right? So what have I got to win or lose?"

He stood up and began to roll his sleeping bag.

"Where are you going?" she asked.

"Out. Going to look for another cabin. If there's one cabin on this lake, there's probably others. Maybe they got more food and some firewood. If we don't find nothin', we'll come back here."

"Can I take my sleeping bag?" she asked.

"Sure, be my guest. Or somebody's, whoever. You should have a warmer jacket. Wait a minute, I had this down vest I was wearing yesterday."

Something jarred her into alertness. "How come you had all these supplies?"

"What supplies?" The contents of his duffel bag were arrayed on the bunk, ready for packing. "Look, kid, I can't afford no fancy hotel. I gotta stay where I can and bring my own stuff."

It didn't look like city stuff to her. Not for a place like Montreal. It was more like camping gear.

"What about the guns?" she asked.

He scowled as he busily packed the duffel. "That shotgun, that's a sample. I sell them things. The other one is for protection. I got a license. People know you're a salesman, they want to rip you off, take everything. Especially that there shotgun." He slipped the gun into his rolled sleeping bag.

She climbed up the ladder and took the other sleeping bag. As she lifted it down, more mouse droppings fell out. She tried not to think about it.

She felt as though her brain were floating away, not part of her. Maybe it was hunger. Or confusion. She hadn't eaten anything since breakfast yesterday, and then she had been too excited for more than a small bowl of cereal. She didn't feel like eating even now. Her stomach wasn't hungry, but her brain floated.

He checked the cabin for anything else that might be of use and pocketed a can opener. "Never can tell," he muttered. She thought that if a place had cans it would probably have an opener, but he was right. You never could tell.

When he pulled open the door, a cloud of snow blew in. She stood in the middle of the floor with the sleeping bag rolled under her arm. He looked back at her and glared.

"What are you waiting for?"

She could feel the iciness even where she stood. "It's so cold."

"It's going to get cold in here, too, baby. The fire'll go out. You'll have to chop more wood. You won't have nothin' to light it with." He tossed something up in the air and caught it. His cigarette lighter. She was at his mercy.

She shuffled toward him and bowed her head as she went out into the wind. It burned her face. It blew through her jeans and through the sleeves of her jacket. She stuffed her hands into her pockets, the bedroll still under one arm. She heard him carefully closing the door, pushing snow out of the way, but she couldn't see him because snow was blowing in her eyes.

Without raising her head, she could watch his legs pushing through the drifts. Already her hands were stinging with cold. She remembered the gloves she had left in the plane.

And her father.

The windshield had been broken. He was probably covered with snow by now. She could almost see him, a snow-shrouded figure slumped against the door. And that woman in the back seat. It would blow in and cover her, too. Again she felt grateful that her father was not alone. She had not wanted the woman, but now was glad of her presence.

The cold would preserve them. Until spring. She did not want to think about that.

The snow had blown so much that in some places the ground was barely covered. In others there were high drifts. Even the edge of the lake was obscured by snow. She knew they were on it when she slipped on ice. At other times she stumbled over small stones.

For a while they followed the shoreline. Then they had to climb high above it, because it rose in a sheer cliff straight from the water. The trees were some protection from blowing snow, but not much. She had thought she would never be warm again. Now she found herself sweating as they climbed higher and higher through the snow and wind.

She was exhausted. She could barely move. Her head grew light. She hadn't eaten in days. Couldn't remember how many days.

She looked ahead and didn't see him any more. Couldn't see anything but bushes all around her, laurel trees, their leaves dry and dark. The sky and the earth were the same dull white. She stumbled and fell and she couldn't get up.

She struggled. Her legs wouldn't lift her. The snow began to blow over her. So cold. With numbed hands she placed the bedroll beside her and lay down, pillowing her head.

15

It was Thanksgiving morning. Ellen had thought she could sleep for a while, but again Natalie woke her.

"Mommy, Daddy, it's snowing!"

Mike raised his head and looked out of the window. "Gawd," he said.

"Is it bad?" Ellen asked, her voice husky with sleep.

"It's a blizzard, just like they promised."

"But what about dinner? Mom and Dad are supposed to come!"

"Honey, we're right in town. The plows are probably out already." He sat on the edge of the bed and pulled aside the curtain. Their whole backyard was buried, drifts piled against the garden shed, and it was still coming down.

"I hope Diane wasn't planning to come today," he said. "I thought she'd be here yesterday, but if she put it off, she's outta luck."

"Why would she put it off?" Ellen asked irritably. She felt irritable every time he mentioned Diane. "I thought Kevin meant something to her."

"I dunno. I don't understand it. She hasn't even called."

Ellen threw the covers aside, exposing her filmy night-gown. "Maybe he doesn't mean anything. Maybe she's got a new boyfriend."

She waited for Mike to turn around and admire her. He continued to stare out of the window. Natalie came back to their room, her hands full of snow that she had scraped from a windowsill. "Can I go out and play?"

"It's too windy," Ellen snapped. Natalie noticed the atmosphere and drove in her wedge.

"Daddy, can I go out? Can I? Please? I'll stay out of the wind."

"Maybe later," he replied.

"When Daddy shovels," said Ellen, "so he can watch you. This is a real storm, honey."

Mike asked, "Are you going to the hospital?"

Her mouth opened. "I have to get the dinner ready!"

She didn't want to go. Oh, how she didn't want to go and see Kevin lying there.

He stared at her, shocked. "You can't just leave the kid!"

Diane's kid. She felt a rush of anger. "It isn't as if they're not looking after him. And what's the point, when he doesn't even know I'm there?"

"He might. You don't know. I think it always helps."

"Well, Diane should get here. I have enough to do. I have the turkey to cook and all the dinner to fix."

"Ellen—"

She did not notice the warning tone. "And besides," she went on, her voice rising, "there's a blizzard out there, and you want me to drive to the hospital. I might get *killed*."

"I'll drive you, dammit. Look, honey, it's only decent, and we certainly owe it to Diane."

"I've been paying," Ellen said through clenched teeth, *"all my life."*

"What the hell are you talking about?" He looked indignant. Still only thinking of Diane and what they had done to her.

"She was always the big, strong one," Ellen said. "The one they counted on. They never *allowed* me to be big and strong. I could have amounted to something, if they'd just let me."

"Mmm." Clearly it was a new thought for him. And clearly he was unimpressed by it. Probably he, too, thought she was a frail ninny who needed sheltering.

He was watching her with an odd expression. No doubt wondering about the time that had produced Natalie. (She hadn't meant to get *pregnant,* for God's sake. She had thought the odds were too high against it.) Probably he wondered whether that, too, had been a result of her jealousy rather than a genuine feeling for him.

"I guess I did end up with the prize." She laughed nervously. "Two prizes. You and Natti. What time is it? I'll call Mom in a little while and see if she's going."

Mike went out with the snow blower to clear the front walk and the driveway. Ellen phoned her mother, only to hear more about Diane.

"I wonder what happened," Marian said. "She told me she'd be on the next plane. That was Tuesday night."

"Maybe she couldn't get a reservation," Ellen suggested. And that was another thing. She was such a hick, she had never been on an airplane in her life, while Diane flew back and forth all the time.

"She'd have called, wouldn't she?"

"Does she ever?" asked Ellen.

"But a thing like this."

"I don't know why everybody's so worried. She'll show up when she gets here. Are you going to the hospital, Mom? Mike thinks somebody ought to go, and I—"

"As soon as we get the driveway cleared. I'll meet you there."

"But—"

Ellen had hoped her mother would be enough representation. She dared not say more. If Marian, at her age,

111

could travel a far greater distance through the blizzard, no one would see why Ellen couldn't, especially as she already had the turkey in the oven and Mike was doing the driving. No one would understand what it did to her to see that ashen, dead-looking little face. Even Marian, who knew the truth, couldn't grasp how important it was for Ellen to try to forget it ever happened.

Besides, there was always the danger that if she refused, Mike might decide to go in her place. He might, by some long chance, be there when Kevin woke and started talking about the accident.

If Kevin woke.

She shuddered. It was a terrible dilemma for her. It would be terrible either way. She did not want him to die, but she did not want him to talk. Mike would hate her forever if he found out how Kevin got hurt. Thank God Natalie had been easily quieted. But she hadn't really been paying attention.

Mike drove her to the hospital, although she insisted she could do it herself. She hadn't wanted to, but that didn't mean she couldn't. He was babying her again. They always babied her.

Marian was in the downstairs lounge. She stood up when Ellen came in and frowned slightly. Ellen recognized the concerned frown she always wore when she knew her very important ideas would not be met with enthusiasm.

"I wonder if we even ought to have a big dinner this year," Marian said. "It just doesn't seem right."

"For cris'sake, Mom, I've already got the turkey cooking. What am I going to do with a twenty-two-pound turkey? Anyhow, it's not going to make a bit of difference to Kevin what we do, but what about the rest of us? What about Natti? She's been looking forward to it."

Natti really had no idea what Thanksgiving was, only that it was a big occasion and her grandparents were coming.

They exchanged long looks. She knew Marian was remembering about the accident.

"Well," said Ellen defensively, "it isn't as if he's dead. Or are you worried about what Diane will think if she gets here in the middle of it?"

"It's hardly that," Marian replied. "I do have some feelings of my own, and it doesn't seem likely that Diane will be coming on a day like this."

Ellen knew how to handle it. She lowered her head. "Well, if you really feel that way, I guess we can always go ahead and eat the turkey, and Natti can watch television, but I know she was looking forward to being with you and Dad."

Marian could not but agree that they had to eat anyway. Besides, there was something noble, wasn't there, about carrying on as usual in the face of tragedy? Or near tragedy.

"Did you drive here?" she asked as they went up in the elevator.

"Mike brought me. He's out parking the car with Natti."

The elevator door opened, and they faced the long corridor to the intensive care unit. Ellen suddenly felt queasy. "Oh, Mom." She reached for her mother's hand.

Marian knew immediately what bothered her. "It's a terrible thing to live with." Somehow that made Ellen feel worse. She almost wished she had kept the whole ghastly secret to herself.

She hung back when they reached the room. She hated the place. Half the people there looked dead already. She hated the tubes and the heart monitors, constant reminders of hovering death. They made the human body into a mere object, a soulless piece of faulty machinery.

Why? she wondered. Why didn't they just let them die, the way nature wanted them to?

"Poor baby," Marian said as she bent over Kevin. Under her hand, he moved his head.

"Did you see that?" she exclaimed, drawing back.

Ellen stared. He wouldn't. He just couldn't. She wasn't ready for it.

Marian reached out again. "Kevin, darling."

He might not remember, Ellen thought, scarcely able to breathe. He might not have understood what happened. But if Mike knew . . .

She had angered Mike enough with the careless things she had done. There was the time Natti had almost drowned in the bathtub while Ellen was on the phone. And the time a broiler fire had set the kitchen ablaze in their former, rented house. The one he had rented with Diane. He might have forgiven her one or two mistakes, but not this. Not when it was Diane's child.

Kevin's head moved again, rolling back and forth on the pillow. Marian beckoned to a nurse. "I think he's coming out of it."

The nurse watched for a moment, checked the monitors, and examined Kevin's eyes.

"It's hard to say," she said. "He might be, but it could take a while. We'll let you know."

"Oh, couldn't we be here?" Marian pleaded. "If he's waking, he should be able to see us, somebody he knows. He's only a baby."

Kevin's eyelids fluttered quickly, and opened. He stared into space, seeing nothing. "Kevin! Kevin, sweetheart!" Marian stroked his face, forcing her living presence on him, trying to pull him back with human contact.

"Mom, we have to go," Ellen said.

"But he's just waking! Hi, Kevin. Hi, baby. You've been asleep. Your mommy's coming to see you."

Kevin's blue eyes fastened on his grandmother. In long, breathy syllables, he repeated, "Mommy?"

"She's coming to see you. She's coming up from New York as soon as she can get on an airplane."

"Mommy?" The voice was firmer, the cry more desperate.

"She's coming, honey. She'll be here very soon."

Ellen moved over so that she stood in front of Kevin, easing her mother and the nurse away. "It's Auntie Ellen, honey. You're looking so much better, sweetie. You're getting all well for Mommy, and Auntie Ellen, and Grandma. We have to go now, but we'll be back later to see you again." She nodded to her mother. "I'll be along in a second, Mom."

Marian complied to the extent of backing away a few steps. "Do we have to go?" she asked the nurse.

"Well, you see, it's already been more than five minutes." The nurse was young and seemed uncertain. "And there are other patients here. They have to be kept quiet."

They looked back at Kevin, whose eyes had closed again. He seemed almost asleep.

"Oh, no!" gasped Marian, seizing his hands.

"Mom," said Ellen, "You're wearing him out. I really think we should go." She turned to the nurse with an apologetic smile. "Will you help my mother tear herself away? I just want another couple of seconds with Kevin. After all, he's my baby, too."

Tears came into Marian's eyes. Tears, probably, at the devotion of an aunt. Embarrassed, she turned to leave the room. The nurse hovered beside her and then went to help another patient.

115

Kevin was rolling his head again. The oxygen tube was still in his nose.

"That's nasty, isn't it?" said Ellen. "It's nasty to have things stuck up your nose. Do you want me to loosen it just a little so you'll feel better?"

She looked around and saw the young nurse watching her.

Oh, God, she thought. *Oh, God.*

Her mind went blank. She couldn't think anymore. The nurse went to tend a beeping monitor. Ellen quickly loosened the tape that held the oxygen tube in Kevin's nose. His thrashing might pull it out.

But it didn't matter, she told herself. Nothing would happen. It couldn't, just from a little oxygen tube, and he was breathing all right, wasn't he? So she hadn't really done anything.

It was only that she had to do *something.* She would leave the rest up to—God?

Backing toward the doorway, where her mother stood waiting, she blew the child a kiss.

"Good-bye, Kevin."

16

Someone seized her arm and jerked her upright.

"What the hell are you doing?" His snarling face looked into hers. She hated him.

"I—fell," she said.

"You wanna die, layin' there in the snow?"

"I don't care." She felt overpowered by sorrow. She bit down to keep from crying. Her tears would only freeze.

"The hell you do." Clutching her arm, he dragged her forward. She pulled back long enough to grab her bedroll, and then she stumbled along behind him. It wouldn't do any good to tell him she wanted to put her hand in her pocket. He wouldn't trust her.

They plunged on through the white world, with snow blowing into their faces. She closed her eyes against it. With her eyes closed, she lost all sense of space and time. She was simply there. She ached. She was going to die.

She wished they had never come. If her father hadn't changed the day, she would be home now in Cresskill, in her nice warm house, because they couldn't have flown in the storm.

The man pulled her on. Her legs and feet were numb. She could not understand why he wanted her. He had killed people. He couldn't have cared about her.

He shouted something and began to run. They were

going downhill now, but the snow was still deep. Her feet were so cold she could barely move them. She slipped in the snow but couldn't fall down because he was dragging her.

"See?" she heard him say. He released her arm and pushed her forward. She stared, bewildered, at the dark thing in front of them. A large shape. A wall. She saw a window in it.

He took her arm again, and they walked around it until they found the door. It faced the lake. She could tell it was the lake. It was flat and white, but she couldn't see much of it through the falling, blowing snow.

He tried the knob. She heard him mutter. He took out his handgun and shot through the lock. Twice. What if he ran out of bullets?

Again it was freezing inside. But they were out of the stinging snow. A pile of firewood stood next to the stove, but there was no kindling.

He observed the woodpile for a moment or two, apparently hoping some kindling would appear. When it didn't, he prowled around the cabin, grunting his approval at the array of canned foods.

Corned beef hash. For the first time in two days, Shelley felt hungry. Would he let her eat it? Or would he keep it for himself?

Finally he found an old newspaper. "Damp," he muttered, as he crumpled the sheets and tossed them into the stove. He laid the logs on top of them and administered his cigarette lighter. A smoky fire began to smolder. It didn't really catch and it gave no warmth.

He pulled a ladder-backed chair over to the stove and sat down.

"Come here, kid."

She shuffled over to him on feet that had no feeling.

"You cold?" he asked. She nodded.

"I could warm you up," he said.

She stopped breathing.

He said, "Lemme see what you got under that coat."

She was too cold, too shocked to respond. He leaned toward her.

"I bet you got freckles all the way down. I never seen tits with freckles."

It was happening. Her mind put up a wall. It wasn't happening. It was all a dream.

He began massaging his pants. She stared hard at the floor. *Mommy. Daddy.*

She tried to think of something to do. Something to lose his interest. She musn't show fear. Or disgust. They like that, she had heard. A teacher at school had told her. Only a week ago, talking with a group of girls. Had she ever been there? In school?

"The fire went out," she said.

It took him a moment to react. Then he opened the stove. He said "Shit." She kept very still.

"Shit," he said again and finally pulled himself up out of the chair.

"Gotta go out," he said. "You wait here. I'll get a fire going, and then you can warm me up, baby." He made a kissing, sucking sound. She backed away involuntarily. He seemed to like that. He grinned.

"You wait," he said again. "Understand? No funny business."

For a moment she stood with her arms folded tightly, trying to keep warm. It was happening. Happening, like a truck with no brakes, rushing down a hill. She couldn't make it stop.

Then her head snapped back. She ran to the windows. Each window.

He was there. Breaking something off a tree. The snow blew around him like a curtain.

He might not see her. If she could get out the front door—

She looked down at her feet. They would have to move. Her head began to swim with anticipation. She almost forgot about the cold. Carefully watching the window, she grabbed the two cans of corned beef hash and stuffed them into her bedroll. Then she checked him again. He was still there, bending over to dig in the snow.

She pulled open the door. The snow gritted in her eyes. She felt it slide down into her shoes, felt the wind against her skin.

He was still behind the house and she in front of it. She scurried up a low hill into the first cover of bushes. She went on until the cottage was lost from sight. Then she stopped.

Where? she wondered. Where?

The lake. There should be a stream running in or out of it. Would she ever find it, or would it be frozen and buried in snow?

She could not walk on the lake, not yet. It was too flat and he might see her. She discovered something that might have been a path running among the trees and bushes along the shoreline. A path would lead somewhere. To a road? It might be miles away.

She couldn't stand a far walk. She was too cold already and hungry.

She ought to have taken a can opener. Even if she could open the cans, with a rock or something, uncooked corned beef hash did not taste like cooked corned beef hash, but there was no way to heat it.

She could build a fire! There was plenty of wood, and she could get warm.

But she had nothing to light it with.

She sobbed in despair. What was she doing here, anyway? At least the cabin was shelter, and there was food. And then she remembered *him*.

Maybe back to the plane. She could use the radio.

But she had no idea where the plane was. And she did not want to see her father dead and frozen.

"Daddy!" she called into the wind. She began to cry, wiping her tears before they could freeze.

Suddenly she stopped and listened. She had thought she heard a voice.

He was coming after her. She began to walk faster, pushing through the snow. She tried to run.

Maybe it was only the wind she had heard. Or a tree falling. Or something.

She ran until she was exhausted. It was stupid to think she could get away and live. Now she wouldn't be able to find her way back, even if she wanted to. She wouldn't live long out here. And her mother wouldn't know. They would think she had died in the crash, but they wouldn't find her body.

She took a breath to call him. She didn't even know his name.

The lake. She could find her way back along the lake.

If she could find the lake. The path had carried her deeper into the woods. She started back the way she had come.

Now she was going down a hill. She could not remember having climbed one. But she had been running and perhaps hadn't noticed.

Down a hill. The lake ought to have been at the bottom of it, but it wasn't.

"Mister!" she called.

He wouldn't hear her. The snow and the hills would block her voice.

"Mister! Help!"

If only she could find the lake. But it wasn't there. She must have imagined it, the whole lake. The cabin.

She started up another hill. That was the one. On the other side she would surely find the lake.

That hill was steeper and harder to climb. She had to stop and hold onto a tree until she recovered her balance. She thought of calling again, but she could barely breathe.

Almost at the top. There was less snow here. Probably it had blown away. She could see bare rock in some places. She looked up to the crest of the hill and saw another hill beyond it.

She stared, betrayed. It couldn't be. Where was the lake? She felt another sob coming. She pushed on, hoping, just hoping, to find at least a stream between the two ridges. But when she could see over the first, she discovered that the ground barely dipped at all. It was flat and then it started up again. She was climbing a mountain. She had lost the lake completely.

She sobbed again. Her nose began to run and her eyes watered. She climbed on. Maybe she could see something from the top. If only the snow wouldn't get in the way. If only—

She couldn't believe what was at the top. It was the plane. *The plane*. She saw it clearly. The nose with the broken propeller. The windows. The door she had left open.

She ran toward it. "Daddy!" Maybe he was alive after all. She could use the radio. She could huddle inside the plane. She might find matches, a map. She might be rescued!

She had almost reached it, when suddenly—it wasn't a plane. A fallen tree trunk, caught on another tree.

She cried aloud. "No!" She had *seen* it. The windows. The propeller. And none of it was there. Only tree branches.

"Daddy!" she cried. "Daddy, help me!"

She screamed into the wind, her arm wrapped around a tree. If he didn't come and help her, she would die. Maybe he wanted her to die so she would be with him.

She was suddenly afraid. He wouldn't do that to her—or not do it to her. He just wasn't there. Nobody was there.

A gust of wind hit her in the back, rocking her. She realized that her feet were completely gone. She would have to move them. Have to keep going. She trudged on toward the next hill.

The wind seemed to blow all around her, but maybe it had a direction. When she left the cabin it had blown into her face from across the lake. Now it was at her back. What did that mean? She couldn't think any more.

Go forward, she decided. Did that make sense? It didn't seem to. But if the wind had been in her face when she looked toward the lake, maybe she could keep it in her face and find the lake again.

Or maybe she was beyond the lake.

She started back down the hill. She could not see anything under the snow, and she slipped on a rock and fell, but the snow cushioned her fall.

She fell again and slid partway down the hill. She hadn't realized it was so steep. Seeing the airplane at the top had kept her going. Again she relived her shock when she discovered it wasn't the plane.

At the foot of the hill, the snow was deeper. Her legs felt raw. Her feet felt nothing. She lost the wind and had to wait until it gusted again. It was stupid to think she could find the lake. But it didn't make any less sense than going on the other way, climbing that endless mountain. Even when she reached the top, she would not be able to see anything in the falling snow.

Was it still falling, or only blowing? She looked up and it fell into her face.

She could lie down again and have it over with. But she was too cold. Not sleepy. She had always thought it sounded like a pleasant death, but it wasn't pleasant at all. It was horrible, being so cold. She would have given anything for a hot summer day. She tried to imagine the beach, the scorching sun. She could not imagine sunshine. It was as though she had never known it.

A thicket of bushes blocked her way. She hadn't seen it earlier. She was lost.

The thicket was too wide to go around. She started to push her way through it. The twigs scratched her frozen hands, drawing blood.

She whimpered aloud. And then was silent. A man stood at the other side of the trees. An old man, with a fishing rod over his shoulder. Ice fishing. She was near the lake! He had his back to her, and he wore a blue-and-black checkered coat and high boots.

"Mister!" she called to him. "Mister, where's the lake?" She stumbled on through the bushes and emerged, bleeding, on the other side.

It was not a man at all. Only the stump of a tree.

Not a man. Not even a fishing rod.

She had thought she saw his back, not his face, but she had known he was old. She had seen a blue-and-black coat where there was only gray.

I'm crazy, she thought. *I'm crazy*.

She began to cry again, sobbing aloud. There was no one to hear her. She was alone in all the Adirondack Forest. Alone in the snow. She was dead, and she wished she could lie down again as she had before and feel the peace, but it was gone. Death was cold and frightening.

She looked back. She had lost the wind again. Maybe it was stopping. And then what? She needed the wind, although it felt better without it. Her feet were lumps of stone.

She started forward, looking back once more at the stump that had been a man. If she could get over that next rise, she might see the lake.

Or might *think* she was seeing the lake, and it wouldn't be true. She might be seeing the sky. How would she know?

Past the rise there was a dip and then a wide expanse of snow without any trees. She knew it wasn't the lake because it rose upward. Or maybe it was the lake. She couldn't trust herself any more.

She walked on, stumbling and sliding. She couldn't catch herself. Her hands were frozen, one stuffed into her pocket, the other into the bedroll. The snow would tear them. Cold flesh tore easily.

She started up over the bare place and found it even steeper than it looked. And slippery. She had to take her hand out of her pocket. She saw that her fingertips were white. Frostbite. She began to cry again.

"Is anybody there?" she called. "Anybody? Help me!"

She fell, landing on one knee. With her legs so numb, she hadn't felt it coming. She pushed herself upright and resumed her climb. Sweat ran down her back inside her clothes.

And then suddenly, up at the top—a figure in a long

white coat. Maybe a nun. The coat was fluttering in the wind. The figure stood with an arm outstretched, feeding the birds. To the right of it was a small house. No, there were two—three houses. Little cottages, painted white. One had smoke curling from its chimney. She began to run, scrambling uphill in the steep snow. She fell and ran again. She was nearly exhausted, but if she could reach the cottage with the fireplace, she could be warm. She could rest.

For some reason, the nun didn't seem to see her. Shelley called, "Hello! Hello, there, Sister?"

Maybe it wasn't a nun. Maybe it was only—

The snow. It was the snow playing tricks on her. The houses were all snow. Even the smoke. They all dissolved into the snowy hillside when she came close to them.

"No," she wept. "Don't go away!"

They had never been there. She was still alone in the Adirondack Forest. She fell onto her knees again. Maybe she could stay there. She looked down and saw how far she had come. How steep it was. She had climbed all that way. If it hadn't been for the houses, she might not have done it. Maybe God put them there so she would climb the hill, because maybe on the other side was the lake.

Only a few more feet. Maybe ten, or twelve, or twenty feet. She couldn't tell. Even the distance would play a trick, and there wouldn't be any lake.

She crawled the rest of the way, and then she reached the top. She looked out into space and saw the snow falling.

She looked down. She was on top of a cliff. Its rocky face dropped into the falling snow. She couldn't see the bottom of it. Only snow.

It's pretty, she thought.

The wind had stopped blowing. She was on top of the

world, in falling snow. Since there was nothing but space and snow in front of her, she had no place to go. For a while she sat and watched the snow. She could watch it forever, that hypnotic, falling snow. From time to time she thought of getting up and walking again.

She couldn't go back the way she had come. She knew there was nothing in that direction. And so she began to walk along the edge of the cliff.

Or maybe she only thought she was walking.

17

Diane listened to the wind outside their igloo. What inspiration had made her think of building it? Or was it Travis? She couldn't remember.

They lay with their bodies pressed together, giving each other what warmth they could. Beside her a small fire flickered. She watched it carefully to be sure it did not melt the roof.

There were two sources of heat, the fire and Travis's body. She felt almost warm. Almost comfortable, compared with last night, in spite of the hard ground and the scratchy pine boughs.

Whenever he stirred, she jumped guiltily, hoping she had not hurt him or made him uncomfortable.

"Is it your chest?" she asked.

"Everything."

She had examined the wound to see whether it was infected. She couldn't tell, nor could she tell how bad his fever was. He seemed very lethargic. His breathing was labored. She felt helpless and guilty. She had gotten him into this, and she couldn't do anything for him now.

She looked out through the smoke hole in the roof. The sky was heavy and gray white. She could not tell whether it was still snowing, or merely blowing. Could they last another night?

"Travis? How are you feeling?"

He groaned. "Don't ask."

"Is there anything I can do?"

He said, "Bring me another pillow and turn down the TV."

She rested her head against his cheek.

"Not funny?" he asked.

"Not funny." But maybe he needed it.

She said, "Tell me about Brazil. Was it warm there?"

"Most of the time. About like this."

"Like—?"

"Here. Right now."

"It isn't that warm, Travis. It must be your fever."

"And you."

"Do you mind my being so close?"

In answer, he tried to tighten his arm around her. He winced in pain.

She said, "I wish I were a doctor."

His jaws were still tight as he answered, "Stockbroker's good enough."

"But I feel so stupid."

"So do I, Diane. Anyway, you built a very competent igloo. How many doctors could do that?"

In her lightheadedness it seemed important to answer the question, but she couldn't. They had to keep talking or they would die.

"Did I show you Kevin's picture?" she asked. Her purse was beside her. She had brought it from the plane. She felt lost without it.

"Show me again."

She took it out and held it up to him. The light inside the igloo was dim and his eyes seemed dim, but she knew he could imagine how Kevin looked. Like himself.

"Gives a guy a funny feeling," he said. "All this time . . ."

"I was afraid you'd think I wanted something from you."

"Why not?"

"What do you mean?"

He closed his eyes. It was an effort to keep talking.

She said, "I thought about you a lot. I couldn't help it with Kevin right there, and I remembered how you came at the right time. You were good for me."

A muscle twitched in his face. "Not good now."

"You are good for me now. My God, if I were alone, I'd go crazy."

"No good."

"Travis, it's good just having you here. I'd be terrified by myself. And you knew how to build the shelter and the bed and everything."

"Same here. Good having you."

"I wish I could do something."

"Just stay."

She supposed that he, too, wanted a live human being for companionship.

After a while he said, "I thought about you, too."

"You did?" It startled her, the voice coming from a nearly unconscious form. And she hadn't imagined that he thought about her at all.

"Thought about. No good at writing letters."

"Neither am I."

Even a postcard would have been welcome. How was she to know he had thought about her?

"Well, here we are," he said. "Together."

"I wish it were different."

"I don't." He spoke drowsily. "Except for this damn—I think it's great being in an igloo with you."

She snuggled closer to him. She would like it, too, if they

were not cold and starving and he in need of medical help.

"At least," she said, "it snowed. If it hadn't snowed—"

"Diane, you're full of 'ifs.'"

"I know."

"You're afraid to accept."

"How can you accept this?"

"Don't have much choice, is what I mean."

She thought she knew what he meant. It did not mean giving up. It had more to do with endurance. You just endured, because what else could you do?

Again his breathing sounded labored. Afraid that she might be pressing on his chest, she lifted herself away from him and looked out through the igloo's entrance. The snow was still falling but more lightly. The entire sheet of bedrock was swathed in white.

She looked back at Travis. He seemed to be sleeping. She tucked the space blanket closer around him. "I'm going out to clear off the signal fire," she said.

He mumbled something vague and assenting. She crawled outside and made her way to the edge of the rock. She discovered the snow was not deep on the exposed rock. Most of it had blown away. The cold stung through her cotton jeans, but her feet were protected by a pair of high-heeled cowboy boots.

She found the fire and shook the snow off the pine boughs that covered it. One more day and night of snow and it would be completely gone. She would have to dig a trench around it.

She could not see through the falling snow. Couldn't see over the side of the mountain to where a lake had been yesterday.

She wondered again about the fire tower. It must have been somewhere near the lake. At least she had seen them both as the plane was coming down. Surely there was no one there in a snowstorm, but there must be a telephone. And it might be connected. It might be their only chance.

But if she set out to look for it, she could easily become lost and Travis would freeze to death. She went back to the igloo.

He lay with his head turned away from her. In the short time she had been outside, his breathing had changed. It was shallow and uneven. She felt a chill that was entirely separate from the weather.

"Travis?"

He didn't answer. Maybe it was better to let him sleep. If he was sleeping.

She added another stick to the fire. When it caught, a flame leaped up to the curved dome of the igloo's roof. She pulled the stick away.

18

The world for Shelley was a dream of falling snow. She moved through it mechanically. Her brain was detached from the rest of her.

How long since she had left the cabin? An hour? Two? Maybe six or eight. Eventually her snowy world would be enclosed in darkness.

On and on. When she wanted to fall, she remembered the corned beef hash. Solid cans of it still in her bedroll. It was the thought of the corned beef hash that kept her going. She couldn't starve as long as she had it.

Suddenly the world spread out before her. Flat, white, and going on forever until it was lost in snow and haze. She stopped and stared, thinking it was another trick. She walked forward until she was almost there. It didn't disappear. It really was. She had reached the lake.

"Ya-hoo!" she cried.

Which way? The lake could be miles around. Twenty or thirty, perhaps. Or maybe only a few.

She walked on, following the shoreline. She could tell roughly where it was, because the flatness ended and the hills began. She walked on the ice, certain that it would hold her. The walking was easier there.

Maybe she was going in the wrong direction. Maybe the cabin was the other way. Wasn't it? At least she was on the lake.

Or maybe it was another lake.

She wouldn't think about that. She would walk around it until she found a cabin. There would have to be something. In summer the Adirondacks were full of people. They needed a place to live, and there were cabins on the lakes.

Something ahead of her loomed large and dark. Another hill, she thought. A mountain. Too small to be a mountain.

Then it was not directly ahead of her but to her right. Its lines were straight and squared.

She turned away. She would not fall for it this time. She had seen houses before, even smoke from a fireplace. She had been within yards of shelter, only to have it vanish. Now she could smell the fire, too. It wasn't fair that her mind should do this to her.

She smelled the fire and saw a window. She had seen the windows on her father's plane. She would not believe it. They couldn't fool her this time.

She stood directly in front of it. She could see a door. If she walked a little closer and reached out her hand, the door would disappear.

The windows looked dark. Of course there wasn't a light on, but she could smell the fire. She took a step closer. Held out her arm. Still too far away.

Another step. Why didn't it go away? It knew she was almost ready to touch it. The others had all disappeared when she was ready to touch them.

Entranced, she moved still closer. It was like playing a game. The house was playing chicken with her. Waiting until she was almost upon it when, like a soap bubble, it would simply not be there. It looked very solid. But so had the others, although she had not thought about solidity then. She had only thought of warmth.

When she was nearly at the window, she could see him

134

inside. It was part of her dream, like the nun and the man with the fishing rod. She could knock and see what he would do. Maybe he wouldn't let her in. But she could go in anyway, because he was only a dream.

She was cold, so cold. She had to get in. She reached for the doorknob. Just a regular knob. It was so cold it burned her hand. But she couldn't stop. She had to get in. She turned the knob and opened the door.

He was working over the stove when she went in. He looked up, glaring.

"Shut that door," he said.

She closed it quickly. He returned to poking at the stove. She watched him, wondering why he didn't say something, or throw her out.

"I took the corned beef hash," she said.

He fastened the door of the stove and brushed off his hands.

"I still have it," she said. "It's here."

She could scarcely move her hands as she pulled the cans out of her bedroll. He did not take them from her. She put them back on the shelf. She was no longer hungry.

"Are you going to let me stay?" she asked.

He shrugged. "It's up to you. If you want to go out there again—"

"I don't."

"Had enough?"

"I never want to go outside again. Ever." She didn't care what else happened. She sat on her bedroll near the stove. "This fire feels so good."

He looked at her, his face reflecting nothing. After a while he said, "We're a long way from nowhere, baby."

"Yes, I know."

"So what did you go out there for?"

"I—"

"You thought you could walk somewhere from here? That's real smart, isn't it?"

He was right. She had been stupid. She had only wanted to get away. He should know that.

"You gotta remember one thing," he said. "I didn't have to let you come with me. It was your idea. If you stayed up at the plane, you'd be dead by now. I saved your life, didn't I?"

"I guess so."

"You guess what?"

She was not sure what he wanted. "You saved my life," she said.

"Right. You just remember that, kid, when I want you to do anything around here. You remember how I coulda left you up at the plane. You'd be dead, if I did. I coulda put a bullet through your head."

Do anything around here. She knew what *that* meant. She couldn't look at him.

"You go to school, kid?"

She nodded.

"You learn things in school?"

Again she nodded. Learn—what?

"You're gonna learn something right now," he went on. "You're gonna remember what really happened when we crashed. You got it wrong, and you owe it to get it the right way. You owe me that much, anyway."

She thought back to the crash. Nothing was happening until he ordered them to land. And he had a gun. She remembered her father swearing, saying they couldn't land there.

Her feet and hands were beginning to ache as they thawed. She remembered how her mother used to run cold water over her hands to ease the pain. She didn't think it had worked very well, but if she could only be back with her mother—who probably thought she was safe in Plattsburgh. And her grandparents, unless they expected them yesterday, would have assumed they weren't coming because of the storm.

"Do you read me, kid?"

She flinched. It sounded like aviation talk. The kind her father used on a plane's radio. And he was gone, because—

"Don't you remember that funny noise in the engine? And your dad wanted to land on them rocks, and I told him we couldn't make it? He wouldn't listen to me."

"My dad—"

She didn't want to make him angry. If she pointed out the truth, he would be angry.

"What about your dad?"

"I don't know."

"What do you mean, you don't know? I just told you what happened. You still got it wrong. Close your eyes and think."

Her hands—the pain—

"You remember? We just crossed that thing, that Lake Whaddayacallit."

"Sacandaga."

"We just crossed that, right? A little piece of it we crossed. Then we started hearing this rattle, like something was coming loose. Your dad said, 'Jesus, what's happening?' Then it got worse. A kind of knocking."

A knocking. She almost remembered. She kept her eyes closed and held her breath against the pain.

"Remember that knocking? That tuk-tuk-tuk-tuk-tuk?"

"Yes."

"Like something was coming loose. He said it was, I

don't know, the fan belt or something. He said we had to land so he could fix it. You got that?"

"I think so." She gasped, wanting to clench her hands, but unable to move them.

"I said, 'You're crazy, you can't land here, there's nothin' to land on.' Remember?"

She nodded. She thought it was her father who had said that, but her father— her father— That terrible knocking. He would have wanted to fix it.

"I said, 'Even if you get down without wrecking the plane, you'll never get back up again. There's no runway.'"

Which was true. They hadn't gotten down without wrecking the plane.

"Wasn't I right?"

She looked up quickly. He had read her thoughts.

"We'da done better to keep going to the next airport," he told her. "At least we mighta had a chance. Answer me, kid. Was I right?"

"Yes. You were." It was safer to agree with him, in spite of her doubts.

"I won't say nothin' against him. He's your dad. But it was bad judgment, right?"

"I guess so."

"Say it louder. Right?"

"Right."

"That's better. Now you tell me what happened. Right from the time we crossed that lake thing."

She almost forgot the pain in her hands and feet. She felt as though her head was spinning and would never stop. She stared at the man. Maybe he was part of those dreams she had had when she was out in the snow.

"I don't know your name," she said.

"I told you when we was back at that airport in Jersey. Arnold Dearborn."

"How did you get on our plane?"

"I asked if I could hitch a ride. I had to get to Montreal. My wife is sick there."

"You told me you killed some people."

"An accident."

"How could you have an accident like that?"

"This kid," he said, "she moved."

"What kid?"

"In the store. There wasn't even money in it. Not much, in a fried-chicken store. Now I'm up to my ass in trouble, just because she moved."

"What's that got to do with your wife being sick?"

"Look, kid, don't get funny with me. I didn't say it had nothin' to do with it. That was an accident. I told you, it was an accident. Understand?"

She wanted to understand. All of it. She wanted to know who he was and why her life had become entangled with his.

"How did the accident happen?"

His lips tightened. He was watching her, but he seemed to be thinking about something.

Then he said, "I'm a cop, see? There was this guy robbing the store. I tried to get a shot at him, but some kid behind the counter went and moved and she got hit instead. Okay? Now you know the story."

"I thought you said you were a salesman."

"I never said nothin' like that. I'm a cop, and when I get back, I'll probably get suspended. They always raise a stink when some civilian gets hit."

She still didn't understand. He had said he was a gun salesman. The shotgun.

"You said—" She thought better of pursuing it.

"I said what?"

He stood over her, insisting.

"You said you blew away two cops. But if you're a—"

"That's part of it. They was shootin' at me. I was plain-clothes. They thought I was the—whadda they call it?—the perpetrator."

It sounded crazy to her. Cops shooting at each other. She didn't know whether to believe him, but it seemed better not to argue.

"How are we going to get out of here?" she asked.

"Can't till the snow stops."

"And then what?"

Again he shrugged. "There's gotta be a road somewhere. There's these houses here."

He was a cop. Or so he said. If true, she was safe with him. And the pain had almost gone. The pain in her hands and feet.

But there was another, larger pain. She could not quite identify it. Maybe it had to do with her father. Because he was dead. Something she had done. She hadn't caused his death, but somehow she felt she had done something wrong.

"You're going to remember that, right, kid? The noise in the engine."

The pain became sharper.

"Are you reading me?"

Her father . . . But it wasn't her fault it happened.

"Cat got your tongue?"

The baby-talk expression jolted her awake. She groped for something. Something she was supposed to remember.

"The engine noise," he said. "Tuk-tuk-tuk-tuk-tuk. You was scared when that happened. You thought we was gonna crash."

It *was* her fault. Her father had wanted to land because she was frightened.

But somehow that didn't feel right.

"I wasn't scared," she said. "I trust my father."

"Yeah, right. Well, maybe he done the right thing. Maybe we couldn't of made it to an airport. He knew more about planes than you and me. It just didn't look like a good place to land, and it turned out I was right. Yeah?"

"Yes."

She was still bothered, but she didn't know why.

He walked over to the window and looked out. "Too bad it hadda snow. We could have maybe got out of here today if it wasn't snowing."

"How would we get out?"

"I told you, we'd find a road. There must be a road going somewheres near these cabins, but whatever it is is buried in the snow."

She could get out if she stayed with him. She had tried it by herself, and she would have died if she hadn't found him again.

In a few days she would be out. She would be on her way home.

"You know," he said, still looking out of the window, "you could sue that there company for renting your dad a defective plane."

"Mr. Adams is a friend of my father's."

"Some friend."

"I don't think he did it on purpose. The FAA inspects the planes."

"So sue the FAA. You could get a lotta money. I'd even come and testify for you, kid. I'd say the crash was an accident, not an attempted landing."

"That's nice of you."

"You could put yourself through college."

She had no desire to profit from her father's death, but

141

the man meant well. She nodded and murmured an agreement.

He asked, "You got it straight now, just what happened? They're gonna ask. They'll want to know how come we crashed, but you don't have to tell 'em about your dad wanting to land. Just say we crashed."

"Yes."

"You got everything just the way it happened? You remember when we started to hear the noise?"

"Just after we flew over Great Sacandaga Lake."

"How do you remember that?"

"I just—remember."

"After we flew over the lake. And then we started to come down. You can leave your dad out of it."

That was what bothered her. The fact that her father had been wrong. That she was forced to admit he had been wrong. Now it was all right just to say they crashed. No one would ask her more than that, and it made her feel better that she would not have to implicate her father.

19

Dinner was over at the Corder house. The day was growing darker and snow was still falling.

"I guess you won't have too much trouble getting home," Mike observed to his in-laws. "I can hear the plows. Crazy weather."

"So much for our postprandial walk." Firman Hastings put an arm around his wife. "I never did like having to get up and exert myself after a big dinner."

Marian regarded him with amazement. "Firman, dear, we've taken a walk after Thanksgiving dinner since the year we were married."

"And I never let on." He winked at Ellen, who managed a faint smile in response. She had tried to eat, so they wouldn't ask questions, but they noticed. Marian had wondered aloud if she might be pregnant again. And Ellen had tried to smile at that, too.

Her nerves were stretched tight. What if he died? What if he didn't?

The ringing of the telephone shocked her almost into a faint. Because she didn't move, Marian went to answer it.

"Oh!" she heard her mother say. "Yes, I see. I'll come over. Right away."

The room seemed to dim. Ellen could hardly see across it.

"Was that Diane?" she asked.

"No. The hospital." Marian looked about her as though not quite certain what to do next. "He's started bleeding again. I thought he was getting better."

"Bleeding?" From what? Oh God, from what?

"Internally. I'm going over—"

"Do they—do they know what—"

"I'm going over. The hospital doesn't have any more blood. And the storm—"

"They don't have blood?" Mike stood up quickly, knocking over an ashtray.

"Not his type," Marian said. "It's very rare. They only had a little and they used it all. It's hard to get, and with the storm— Oh, I *wish* Diane were here."

"She's not coming in this weather, that's for sure," said Mike.

"Maybe she's taking the train," Ellen suggested.

"I'll call her." Marian grasped at something. Anything. She looked up Diane's number in her address book, dialed, and waited.

"There's no answer. I don't understand. It's been two days. She was coming up on the next plane."

"Probably waiting at the airport," said Firman. "Probably couldn't get a seat, with the holiday, and now this storm."

"But she'd have called!"

Ellen said, "Maybe the lines are down."

They glared at her. It must have been a stupid thing to say. But she felt magnificently relieved that Diane could not be reached. "Maybe she went out to dinner."

"Well, I'm going to the hospital," Marian declared. "For all I know, I might have that blood type. Dear, I think you ought to come, too." To Firman.

"Of course."

"I'll get this mess cleaned up," said Ellen. She went into

144

the dining room and began to stack the dessert plates.

Marian called, "Why don't you leave the dishes? I'll come back and help." But she didn't mean it. She was busy putting on her boots and would probably spend the rest of the day with Kevin.

"Anything I can do?" Mike asked them. "I could drive you over. Then you wouldn't have to park. They don't have much of the parking lot cleared."

They were all in a dither. Because it was Diane's child. They felt they owed her the universe. Guilty, guilty, guilty. For what?

I'm the one who did it, Ellen reminded them—but never aloud. I'm the one who took Mike away. Because *she* owed *me*, for always being the strong one.

She had wanted him to fall in love with her. She hadn't meant to get pregnant. It was messy and embarrassing. She had only wanted him to change his mind and tell Diane he had found his true love. She still cringed when she remembered that horrible dinner after Diane's graduation, when they told her. If only Diane had crumpled or cried or done something to make herself look weak. Instead she had maintained an icy calm and had called Ellen a whore. If anything was guaranteed to make Ellen hate her forever, it was that, because Mike was sitting right there and he was still a little bit in love with Diane, and Ellen could never be sure that statement hadn't made him see her through Diane's eyes.

A *little* whore. That was what she called her. Not just a whore, which might have betrayed a certain amount of envy. A *little* whore.

Then she had walked out of their lives, but not out of Mike's mind.

Mike wandered into the dining room. He hadn't driven them after all. He wore a gray three-piece suit, but had taken off the jacket. He looked gorgeous. He carried the pies out to the kitchen and wrapped them in plastic.

"Do these go in the refrigerator?" he asked.

"Mom always puts them there."

He opened the refrigerator and began to clear a space for the pies. "I wonder what happened with the kid. That'd be rotten for Diane if—"

"If Diane cared, she'd have been here yesterday. Or at least she'd have called."

His look was stern, but his voice was mild. "You know better than that, hon."

"Better than what? She isn't here, is she? As Mom said, it's been two days."

"And as your dad said, she probably had trouble getting a flight, because of the holiday."

"Then why hasn't she called?"

Mike scowled. In his book, such dereliction was not typical of Diane. "Maybe something happened."

"Like what?"

It was a challenge. He wavered. "Well, she's in New York. Anything can happen there."

"You know damn well nothing happened. And you can bet if it was Natti lying there in the hospital, you can bet I'd come by dog sled, if I had to."

He said nothing. Undoubtedly he was thinking that Diane would, too.

And maybe he was wrong. Maybe Diane was not as strong, or responsible, or steadfast as everyone believed.

"I wouldn't be surprised," said Ellen, "if she wasn't even married when she had Kevin."

"So?"

"Well, I think she wasn't. He was probably already married."

"So, what does that prove?"

She winced. If it was true, then even there Diane had been stronger than she was. She had taken Diane's fiancé to provide her own child with a father, while Diane had gone through with it alone. There didn't seem to be anything she could do or say that would dim the luster of Diane's image or improve her own.

"Are you still in love with her?" Ellen asked.

"God, how many years have we been married?"

"Five. And that's got nothing to do with my question."

"Look, honey—"

"You were in love with her first. And you only married me because you got me in trouble."

A flush suffused his cheeks and then receded. He stood looking at her, biting his lip, his eyes narrowed. She felt her heart beginning to pound with mortification and a kind of fear as they both remembered that spring vacation.

"You talk as if I seduced you," he said.

"Well—it was both of us."

"It certainly was."

"I loved you, Mike. I wanted you."

"I wanted you, too."

"More than you wanted her?"

"She—" He stopped and decided not to say whatever it was. "How come you're so jealous of her?" he asked. "Is it just because of me?"

"I'm not jealous."

"You're jealous as hell. It's eating you up, and it doesn't make sense. It should be the other way around."

How could she explain? She wasn't sure herself.

"Maybe it's because she didn't have anything wrong with her when she was born."

He burst into raucous laughter. "Good God, kid, you

haven't got anything wrong with you now except your god-damn jealousy. Nobody carries a thing like that—"

They both jumped as the telephone rang.

"Diane," said Ellen.

Mike was closer and he picked it up. She watched his face drawing together in a sober frown. It wasn't Diane. He wouldn't have looked that way for Diane.

He lowered the phone. "It's your mother. They want you over at the hospital."

She felt her face go pale. "What for?"

"Just a test. Your mom can't remember what kind of blood you have."

A test. Give Kevin her blood. Did she owe Kevin her blood?

"I'll drive you there," he said. "Natti and I'll wait down-stairs."

"I don't—"

"You have to do it, honey. He needs the blood, and they can't get any in because of the storm."

"What if I don't have the right kind?"

"I don't know what then. Maybe they'll have to appeal on the radio, or something."

The thought of giving blood revolted her. She did not want to see Kevin or the hospital, but there was no way out of it. Slowly, scarcely able to move, she bundled up Natti in her snowsuit and boots.

In the bathroom she prayed. It was the only place where she could be alone.

"God forgive me for what I did. God forgive me for *everything*, but just don't let me have Kevin's kind of blood."

It was not only the idea of giving blood. She did not want it to go to Kevin. Her blood in Diane's child. And it might help him to live, and then Mike—

But if he died—

Her confusion was giving her a headache. They went out to the car, and Mike drove slowly to the hospital, three miles away. She was sent immediately to the second floor, a little room that looked out on snowy trees. She closed her eyes while her arm was pricked. "I hate this," she said weakly to the technician and felt that she would throw up.

But her prayers were granted. She did not have AB negative blood.

Her parents had joined Mike and Natti in the waiting room. It was not until she saw their faces that she remembered what this was all about.

She had been their last hope. And again, of course, she had disappointed them.

"I didn't think you had it," Marian said dully. "I think I would have remembered." She buried her face in her hand.

Ellen said, "Well, somebody must have it. Diane, or the baby's father, wherever *he* is. I can't understand why Diane—"

She was stopped by a look from Mike. She still maintained that Diane had had plenty of time to get there before the snow, but the others were beginning to feel that something must have happened. Now they worried not only about Kevin but Diane, too. What could happen, Ellen asked herself, that would keep her at least from calling?

"Diane does have it," Marian said. "She told me. And that was another reason—"

"Well, as Mike said, they'll probably put it on the radio."

She had hoped to dispel their gloom, which seemed like a personal assault on her. It had no effect at all.

"The poor little thing," said Marian. Then she glanced quickly and stealthily at Ellen.

Ellen looked away. "What made him start bleeding again?"

Marian shook her head.

"I mean, did anything happen?"

"They didn't tell us anything. Why?"

"I just wondered. I thought he was getting better."

"We all thought so." Marian got up from her chair, slowly, as though it were an effort. "Firman, I'd like to go home and try Diane again. Then maybe we can come back."

"By all means." Firman shook out the storm coat that had been folded in his lap.

Ellen had started to button her own coat, when Mike said, "I think we ought to stay, El. I wouldn't feel right leaving the kid alone now."

She was about to protest, but was squelched by Marian's agreement. "Oh, would you? At least till we get back. We can take Natti with us."

She would just have to stay. And suffer. As if it hadn't been bad enough when she looked behind the car and saw him there. Now all this. It was unbearable. No one seemed to realize how it was for her.

150

20

They went over it again and again, about the engine noise. The plane crash. Her brain felt like a bowl of soup. Something revolting and stringy.

"You got that, kid?"

She stared at the window. "I wish the snow would stop."

"You're not paying attention." His voice was smooth and quiet. "I told you, when we get this squared away, we'll start looking for how to get outta here."

"You said when the snow stops."

"Well, both. But we gotta be ready when the snow stops. We gotta get the story straight, or we'll be in a lot of trouble. You know how they always investigate these plane crashes. If we get it straight, they'll just write it down and it will be all over; but if we mess it up, it could look pretty bad for your pop, understand?"

"Yes."

"And he can't say nothin' for himself."

"I understand."

"So here's what we'll do. You tell me one more time what happened, and then we'll have something to eat. You hungry?"

"Could we have the corned beef hash?"

"Corned beef hash it is. Now you tell me from the time we flew over Albany."

By now, she could hear the engine knocking in her head. Tuk-tuk-tuk-tuk-tuk. That unnerving sound, when they were thousands of feet up in the air. She remembered her terror, and her father trying to reassure her. Then feeling he should land. For her sake. And that voice from the back seat. "Are you crazy? You can't land here."

Seeing the earth rush toward them, the lakes and trees wheeling past. Seeing the boulders, and then the bumping and scraping. She would never forget it. Never.

I was in a plane crash and I survived, she thought.

He told her she was lucky to have survived. But, he said, it wouldn't have done her much good without his help. She would have frozen to death. As it was, as soon as the snow stopped, she would be on her way home.

"It wasn't too long after Albany, was it?"

"A little while. Maybe—half an hour? It wasn't long after we crossed that part of Great Sacandaga Lake."

"Good girl. You know, you're a good kid. How about we bust out the corned beef hash?"

Diane was hungry. It had been days since they had eaten anything. Two days. She thought the second day was nearly over, or maybe it was only the clouds that made it dark. Or maybe she was dying, losing her vision.

They had taken off much of their upper clothing, the better to warm each other. They lay on her coat with his over them, and the space blanket over that. She loved the feel of his body, hot and wasting though it was. She could almost forget the chinks of cold, the chill on her back, the outside temperature, which was probably in the teens or twenties. Travis said it felt colder than it was, because it was early in the season. They weren't used to it yet.

"I'm trying to pretend we're back in my bedroom," she

told him. "Remember my old bedroom, where we made Kevin?"

This time he did not respond at all. He had faded still farther from her. She did not want to imagine how it could end.

"The snow will have to stop tonight," she said.

She could feel his hot, dry breath on her shoulder. She went on talking, to hold him there. She must not let him drift away.

"Tomorrow I'll go and look for the fire tower. I saw a fire tower when we were coming down. I figure they've got to have a telephone, even if nobody's there. I'd go now, but I think it's getting dark. It must be close to evening. We'll just sleep for a while, and as soon as it gets light—"

"Can't—go," he muttered.

"Don't try to talk. I'll do all the talking. Anyhow, I saw this fire tower, and I'll go and look for it in the morning. It was on a hill above a lake."

She was rambling, but it didn't matter, as long as she kept him with her. If he could stay alive for one more day, maybe the search planes would come.

"One more day," she said.

"Mmm?"

"They'll come tomorrow, because the snow will be over tonight. It's letting up right now."

She knew he wouldn't look at it and realize she had lied. She had to give him hope. That was the most important thing.

"We should have brought sandwiches, or something," she went on. Food might have helped him, too. "But we thought we'd be in Massena by noon. And I wasn't hungry. I was too worried about Kevin. Oh, Travis, I wish you could see him. You *will* see him. He looks so like you. The same eyes, and that hair. It's your color hair, not light like Shelley's."

She wished she hadn't mentioned Shelley. But maybe that, too, would give him a reason to live.

Achingly, she thought of Kevin. He might have died in these two days. But that was impossible. Not her boy. Her only child.

Yet it happened to other people. Her heart expanded to take in suffering parents everywhere. She understood now. She would never again read a news story about a hurt, killed, or lost child without understanding.

"If I just hadn't gotten the flu," she continued, "he'd be with me now. We'd be having fried chicken today, just for him. Do you know it's Thanksgiving, Travis? He loves fried chicken. The only trouble is, if he were with me, and I wanted to see you, I wouldn't be able to. I mean, imagine if you came back from Brazil and discovered you had a three-year-old son. If you saw him, you'd know he was yours. I thought boys took after their mothers."

He was asleep. She could tell by the breathing. She would stay awake and watch him, listen to his breathing. The fever might keep him warm for a while, but the infection would only get worse.

And it was still snowing. She could see it even in the growing darkness, the snowflakes falling toward her face. They looked black against the gray sky, but after a while it would be dark and she wouldn't see them at all, but they would still be falling.

Until we're buried here, she thought, and hugged Travis more tightly.

21

It didn't check out.

Jerry Mercer had written down every description from every witness. Most of them tallied, at least in a general way. All except one. It was the best one, too. That cracker-jack witness who remembered so many details. The Wallek girl. His daughter's friend.

He had written each description on a separate sheet of paper. He had made charts to show which person had noticed which characteristic.

"Jerry?" His wife, Doris, stood red-eyed in the kitchen doorway. "Can't you stop now? It's not going to bring her back. You've been at it all day. They've all been at it."

"So it's not going to bring her back," Jerry replied. "Do you want him home free? Listen to this, hon."

He picked up one of the descriptive sheets.

"Nuñez, Rafael. He says steel-rimmed glasses, round lenses. He's sure it was steel. Dark eyes. Looked as if he could knock off his grandmother. Dark straight hair, short in back. Dark mustache. Nothing worn on head. He's sure about that, too. Brown tweed jacket, old and tacky-looking.

"Nuñez, Migdalia. Steel-rimmed glasses. She remembered his eyes were like ice. Says, 'You never saw gold ice.'"

"That doesn't prove anything," Doris said.

"It's the effect you get. She remembered steel. Dark hair. Short. Mustache. Thinnish face. Hard. Cold. Doesn't remember anything worn on head. Wool jacket, brown and white."

"Perkins, Henry. Glasses. Couldn't see his eyes because the light was on his glasses. Dark mustache. Evil face. Dark hair, kinda short. Speckled jacket. No recollection of anything on head.

"Wallek, Gina. Mustache. Gold-rimmed granny glasses. Well-built, about six feet tall. Longish hair that covered his ears, blue knit cap, brown corduroy jacket with elbow patches."

He looked up at Doris. She was standing with her arms folded, listening to him. At least she had stopped crying.

"And?" she said.

"That's it. Notice anything funny about that?"

"Funny?"

"Christ, hon, you know what I mean. Don't you think there's something fishy? One witness sees almost everything different from all the others. Not too different. Just enough so we're not talking about the same thing. Now, is she wrong or are they wrong?"

"Who? Which one?"

She hadn't been listening.

"Here. Come and look at these." He pulled out a chair. When she was seated with him at the kitchen table, he showed her what he had just read.

She studied it for a while, apparently trying to figure it out. Then she said, "Gina? But that was her friend. Of course she'd do her best."

"Honey, look at these other people."

"Who are they?"

"They were customers in the store. He was robbing

156

them, too. He told them to empty their pockets while he went to the cash register."

"I don't want to talk about it." She threw down the paper and got up from the table.

He patted her hand. "I know. I'm sorry, hon. But I'm not going to stop until we find the guy, and I think I'm onto something."

"But Homicide—" It seemed incredible to be applying that word to their own child.

"I know they're working on it," he said patiently. "But I gotta work, too. I can't just sit around."

She sniffled.

He said, "I have to go out for a while."

"Jerry, whatever you do—"

"It's okay. I'm not going to do anything. I just want to talk to somebody."

She followed him out of the kitchen. "Dress warm. And come back soon."

He put on his coat and went out into a wet, slushy snowfall. The sidewalk was a mass of puddles and lumpy slush. He hoped it wouldn't freeze during the night.

He had already ascertained that she was working that day. Fried chicken must be sold, even on Thanksgiving.

He waited, concealed in a doorway near the entrance to Jack's. He hoped she would be coming out alone.

There could be several explanations. Maybe she was a highly imaginative witness. Some were like that. If they couldn't give a description, they invented one and convinced themselves it was real. It made them feel important.

Or maybe she was intimidated. If that was the case, it meant she had some contact with the killer, direct or indirect.

Or maybe—

He backed farther into the shadows as he saw her pushing open the glass door. He recognized her coat, a gray tweed with purple flecks. A purple scarf on her head. She seemed undecided, looking one way down the sidewalk, then the other. And then she started walking.

He waited until she had nearly reached him.

"Gina."

She looked up in total shock.

He said, "You lied, didn't you, Gina? About the description."

Her frosted lips parted. "I— What? What do you mean?"

"The description you gave. You lied, didn't you?"

She stared at him, still feigning bewilderment, but he knew he had reached her. She was too nervous for somebody who had innocently given a faulty description.

"You want to talk about it?" he asked.

He hoped she wouldn't. Not to him, anyway. He didn't want anything that might jeopardize the case.

She said, "Look, Mr. Mercer, I don't know what you want from me, but you're wrong if you think I lied. I loved that kid."

"So did I, Gina."

She rested her hand on his arm. "I know. I want to help. I told you everything I could."

Then she slipped around him and tried to hurry on down the block. His legs were about twice the length of hers. He had no trouble keeping up with her.

"You see, Gina, you gave a very detailed description of the man who shot my daughter, but for some reason, it's a lot different than the other people saw. And they all saw more or less the same thing, even if they don't remember every detail."

"I still don't know what you mean."

They had to stop at the corner for a traffic light. She stared straight ahead, watching the red Don't Walk sign on the other side of the street.

"You don't know what I mean. Well, how can I explain it?"

"I just told them what I saw. I don't know what else I can do. I even found his picture in the mug shots."

"You saw a guy with rimless glasses. That's what you told the officers on the scene."

"That's right."

"I'm sorry, Miss Wallek, it isn't right. You said silver-rimmed."

"I said—I said gold-rimmed. That's what it was. Gold-rimmed."

"That's what you said, or that's what it was?"

"Look, mister." She turned to face him. "I gave the right description. I told them what I saw."

"I'd believe you," he said, "because you had a chance to observe, even under stress, while he went after the customers first. A funny thing, though. The rest of them all agree with each other but not with you."

"So what do you want me to do? Change what I said to match the others?"

"I want you to think about it, Gina. Think about what you're doing. I know you're lying and I know why. We'll get at the truth sooner or later. You know that, even if you were probably told that cops are dumb. It isn't true. We have a lot of brains on the force and a lot of sophisticated techniques, so we'll get there, even if it takes a while. Good night, Gina."

He walked away, hoping he left her breathless. Probably she expected him to follow her home and then hassle her when nobody could see it. He didn't need to. He thought he had made his point. A little bluster, just to start her worrying. If they didn't hear from her in a day or so, then he'd lean on her.

In the meantime it was already two days after the shooting. The trail was getting cold, except possibly for Gina. Becky's funeral would be tomorrow. He had wanted some progress by then.

He kept going back to Gina. He really thought he was onto something.

He had to think, and it was cold out on the sidewalk. He went into a diner and ordered a cup of coffee.

"Some weather we're having," said the girl behind the counter. "First it rains for two days, then the sun comes out and it goes down thirty degrees, and then it *snows*."

"Well, what do you want?" he asked absentmindedly. "It's November."

"Maybe I want July."

He suddenly took a look at her. "Do you live around here?"

"Yeah, why?"

"Do you know a girl named Gina Wallek?"

"No, why?"

"Just wondered." He spooned sugar into his coffee. He had learned two things. He took a notebook out of his pocket to write them down.

One, she hadn't just given a mistaken description. In his view she had been too definite about it. Too sure of herself. He didn't know homicide investigation all that well, but he figured he knew people.

And two, he didn't think she was being intimidated. She wasn't frightened or nervous. Not for herself, anyway.

That left some interesting alternatives.

And maybe he had just wrecked everything by leaving her when he did. Maybe he should get someone to question her right away, before she had time to think. If he could find anyone. And they'd probably tell him to wait till tomorrow. If they went for the idea at all.

He could blow the whole thing by doing it himself. But something told him it had to be now.

He threw a dollar bill onto the counter. "You sure you don't know any Gina Wallek?" he asked the girl.

"I told you."

"Okay. Wish me luck."

"Mister, if you haven't got flowers, take her a doughnut, at least."

Gina Wallek lived in an old brick building, on the second floor. There was no name on the doorbell, but he knew her apartment number. He rang the bell.

Her voice came through the intercom, distorted by static.

"Police," he said.

He guessed it was a front apartment, but he didn't know which one. His quarry could be heading down a fire escape right now. He hadn't come prepared to make an arrest. Either way, he might be missing his chance.

The longer he waited, the more he wished he could see the back of the building, but he couldn't be both places at once. Then she rang the release bell, and he pushed open the door. Interesting. At least she had let him in.

He didn't bother with the elevator, but jogged up the stairs. Apartment 2H was to the right, around a corner. It was a low, sprawling building. Lots of room for fire escapes. He rang the bell.

"Yeah?" She must have been standing right next to the door.

"Police, Miss Wallek."

"Mr. Mercer?"

"You know I'm a cop."

He heard the chain rattling in its slot. A lock being turned. The door opened a crack. He inserted his shoe.

"I'd like to come in, Gina."

"You have a search warrant?" Her voice trembled.

"I'm not searching anything. I just want to talk to you."

"You already did."

She couldn't shut the door because his shoe was there. He asked politely, "May I come in?"

Slowly the door opened. He stepped inside and looked around quickly. He could have been walking into an ambush.

He was in the kitchen. An odd place for an apartment to start. Probably it was part of a larger apartment that had been divided into smaller ones. He could see a door leading into another room. He would have liked to see the other room, and most of all the bedroom, but he had to restrain himself.

"Nice place," he said. "Is your husband out working?"

She didn't have a husband. She lived with a boyfriend. When Becky had finally figured that out from their conversations, she had been bug-eyed. She felt she had really moved into an adult world, exchanging confidences with a woman who had a live-in boyfriend.

"Um—yes," Gina answered.

"What does he do?"

"He, um—does odd jobs."

"When do you expect him back?"

A sullen shrug. "When he gets back, I guess."

"Kinda late, isn't it, for odd jobs?"

"He's a night watchman this week."

"Sounds good. Does he carry a gun?"

162

She paled. "Sometimes."

"Wear a uniform?"

"Yeah."

"And you don't know how late he works."

"I don't know. I'm usually asleep."

"What's the address?"

"Huh?"

"Where he works."

"I don't know. It's just this week."

"You probably have a wedding picture."

"Huh?"

"A wedding picture. You and him."

"Oh, we're not married."

"I see." It was interesting that she hadn't asked him why he wanted to know all these things. In fact, it was probably a significant omission.

He wandered toward the living room and looked in. He saw an overstuffed sofa and a glass-topped cocktail table. A buffet with a faked antique finish. They were probably still paying for the furniture.

A glimpse of a darkened bathroom. So it was a one-room apartment. The sofa would open into a bed.

In an instant he saw all that, and then his eyes moved quickly back to the buffet. Its top was a clutter of knick-knacks, figurines, and a few unframed snapshots propped against the rest of the stuff. He hesitated for a moment or two, then walked into the room.

"Hey!" she called.

He picked up a snapshot. It showed Gina and a man sitting at a table, their faces caught in the glare of a flash-bulb. It must have been a party of some kind. There were garish paper plates and half a balloon showing off to one side.

"That him?" he asked.

"No. That's my brother."

"Your brother, huh? Must be a stepbrother. He doesn't look much like you." The man's face was thin and angular. Hers was round. It didn't matter. At least there was a face to go on now. Some kind of sixth sense told him he was on the right track, even if it didn't much resemble either of the mug shots. Maybe it was a little closer to Arlie Dean.

"Older or younger than you?" he asked. Not seeking information, only a reaction.

"Older."

"Does he live around here?"

"Uh—no, in Jersey."

"Oh, yeah? I have cousins there. Where in Jersey?"

"Um—Newark." Probably the only city she had ever heard of in New Jersey.

"Newark, huh? That's where my cousins live. Anywhere near Walnut Street?"

"I don't know exactly where."

"You don't know his address?"

"I'd have to look it up."

He could see that she immediately regretted having said that. Out of pure meanness, he asked, "Would you do that for me?"

He watched her hands clench into fists. "I don't know why you need my brother's address."

"You never can tell," he said. "Maybe I want to look him up next time I'm in Newark."

The hands uncurled and then clenched again. "Well, he's not there right now. He's in—he's in Alaska."

"I don't envy him," Jerry said genially, "with winter coming." She thought she wasn't telling him anything, but he was learning a lot.

"No, I don't, either," she said, glad to be back on safer ground.

"It was nice talking to you, Gina."

Her face lit up with relief. He could spring a nasty one on her now, but he thought it was better to keep her good will. Anyhow, he had a face. It was seared into his mind, but he took a last look at the picture, just to be sure. He would check the mug shots tomorrow.

"Sorry I barged in on you so late in the day," he added. "Goodnight and pleasant dreams, Gina."

He heard the door lock behind him and the chain slide into place. She had acted as though he'd scared the bejesus out of her, but she was pretty quick with the answers, most of them.

A brother in Newark. He doubted it very much. Even if that was a brother, he was still worth looking into. Whatever the identity of the man in the photograph, he had been wearing wire-rimmed glasses and a mustache.

22

Sometime in the night, Diane woke. She was shocked that she had fallen asleep.

Her arm was around him, her bare skin against his. She lay for a moment, feeling the heat of his body. So hot. She knew he couldn't last much longer.

It was their second night on the mountain. If they could reach their second night without being rescued, then rescue would never come.

The wind had died down. Snow was still falling lightly and quietly. Maybe it would stop soon. But even if the skies were to clear, search planes could not go up until the runways were plowed. By then Travis would be dead.

His breath was hot on her neck. The world was black outside the igloo and inside, too. She knew the snow would not melt until spring. It had covered the plane, which was white anyway. The only thing they would have going for them was the signal fire. And what if they couldn't light it in time? What if it didn't flare up and catch on the oil and rubber?

What if the planes never came?

He would die there in her arms. If only they could die at the same time.

"Travis?" She moved her own body gently, hoping for a

response. She did not know whether it was better to wake him or let him sleep.

"Travis, the snow is stopping."

Maybe in the morning, she thought, trying to believe it herself. Maybe even that morning they would clear the runways and send up the planes.

Or maybe they wouldn't hurry about it, because they would assume that after two days, there would be no survivors. Could they do that? She knew nothing about their procedures, or even who "they" were.

She stayed awake for a long time. Then again, without intending to, she fell asleep.

The sky was beginning to lighten when she woke. Thank God she still felt him breathing beside her. Every hour was important. And thank God another night was over.

Her back felt icy. Her toes were growing numb. She had taken off her boots and his shoes and wrapped their feet together, hoping they could keep each other warm.

"Travis?"

His head rolled back. She gasped. Dead! Then he gave a faint moan. His eyes remained closed.

"Travis, it's morning."

The only answer was the sound of his breathing.

She looked out. It was still too dark to see much, but she thought it had stopped snowing.

She tried to sit up. She could scarcely move. It was too much effort. She wondered how long they could last in the cold without food. They needed food to keep warm.

It's only two days, she thought. You don't starve in two days.

But you could die of hypothermia.

She closed her eyes and lay on their lumpy bed, holding him. She was cramped from being in the same position all night, but she did not want to let go of him, ever.

He drew a long breath that sounded like a sob. She tightened her arms. He mustn't leave her. She felt the stubble on his face against her shoulder.

Another uneven breath. She whimpered impatiently, staring at the sky. Would it never be light?

And then another interminable day. A day of waiting and hoping and losing hope.

She couldn't just let him die. But what could she do?

Stay with the plane, he had told her. The people who survive are usually the ones who stay with the plane.

It was a hard thing not to start walking. He had told her that, too. People want to be doing something. But the ones who walk are often never found. Not even their bodies.

She remembered the fire tower. Oh God, the fire tower. If only she could see it. If they had binoculars.

Which way? There were three hundred sixty degrees all around them. She had no idea where the fire tower had been. Was it before or after they circled to land?

While they were circling, just to make it more complicated. And the lake had been before. The lake was down there. Down the mountainside from where they were now. She had seen it that first afternoon. But where was the tower in relation to the lake?

Maybe if she walked all around. They were high up on something. Not quite on top of a mountain, but on the side of one. If she could reach the top, she could see.

If she could reach the top. She wondered how high it was. From the site of their camp, it was impossible to tell. The ground just seemed to rise.

She might be able to reach the top, if she could walk at all. If she had the strength and the snow were not too deep. They were already well above the base of the mountain, and many of the Adirondacks had high interconnections, like the webbing between the toes of a duck. You could be thousands of feet above sea level, but the distance from base to summit was far less.

She imagined herself climbing to the top. She could probably do it, if she did not encounter cliffs or sheer rock.

But once at the top, she would be nowhere. Even if she could see the fire tower, she would have to walk to it. That would mean leaving Travis alone. She could not tend the fire or keep him warm with her body. And the telephone in the tower might be disconnected. It could all be for nothing. And the snow, at least in places, would be deep after all this time. The walking would be slow and exhausting. Maybe even impossible.

But she could not just sit there and let him die.

She closed her eyes and dozed fitfully to pass the time. She woke abruptly at the ragged sound of his breathing.

Maybe she could try the radio in the plane. Maybe this time she would reach somebody.

She dozed and woke again. It was lighter now. And no longer snowing. The sky was low and gray.

Maybe not too low for search planes.

But there were still the runways to clear. And it looked as though it might snow again.

"Travis?"

He did not answer.

"Travis, it's stopped snowing. I'm going to try the radio."

She waited for a reaction. Anything to show that he was conscious and had heard her. He only lay with his eyes closed, drawing shallow, painful breaths.

She watched him, as prickles of chill inched over her body. There wouldn't be time to climb the mountain. Or anything.

She said, "I'm going outside on that flat place and trample an SOS in the snow. The planes should be along any minute, and they'll see it. Then I'm going to try the radio. I'll be back in a little while."

He remained limp even when she took her jacket out from under him. She dressed herself quickly, then wrapped him in his own jacket and the space blanket, tucking it tightly even around his head.

She worried about the fire. Perhaps the igloo itself and the space blanket would be enough. He had told her of a Siberian Eskimo woman who lay for several days under the snow before she was rescued. She had buried herself, knowing the snow would keep her warmer than the outside air. But she was probably dressed for the outdoors. Travis had expected to spend most of his time in a heated plane.

She crawled out of the igloo and walked back through the woods to the plane. She switched on the battery. This time it made no sound.

Too cold, she thought. Oh my God, it was too cold. She knew nothing about airplanes but assumed it was the same as a car battery. Although knowing it wouldn't work, she picked up the microphone.

"Mayday! Mayday! Is anyone there? Please answer. This is an emergency. Mayday! It's life or death."

She gave the plane's number and the approximate location. She was more precise than Travis had been. "We're north of the eastern arm of Great Sacandaga Lake, en route from Albany to Massena."

It was still not precise enough, but that didn't matter. The message was not being transmitted, much less heard. She repeated it twice, then switched off the power.

With Travis's army knife, she cut some strips from the plastic seat covers. They were beige, not a very conspicuous color, but the best she could manage. She would use them to mark her trail so she could find her way back.

Returning to the igloo, she looked inside. He was exactly as she had left him.

She couldn't believe he might be dying. Not after all those years apart. Not Travis.

She thought: We're a family. Because of Kevin.

Maybe Kevin was gone, too. Maybe both of them together. But what about her?

She made a pretense of tucking the blanket around him once more, so he would know she was there and because she felt so helpless.

"I'll be right back," she told him. He wouldn't know how much time was passing, and he needed hope. She pushed a wall of snow against the entrance to make the opening smaller and keep in more heat.

Wind had blown the snow almost smooth on the field of bedrock, obliterating the footprints she had made yesterday on her several trips to clear the signal fire. She trampled an arrow pointing to the igloo and then a large SOS that covered the entire face of the rock.

It took her nearly to the corner where their signal fire was. Once more she cleared away the snow. She hoped the wind would not start again and destroy everything. She prayed that a plane would fly overhead and see her SOS and the arrow. Or better yet, a helicopter that could land there. It didn't matter about her, as long as Travis was saved. She had never seen anyone die or anyone so close to death. She could not believe how fragile life was.

She walked back along the edge of the bedrock, so as not to disturb her message, and into the forest and began to climb the first slope.

The snow was deep. She realized at once that it would take her hours to climb even a little way. She was crazy. Stark mad. The goose down kept her shoulders warm, but her jeans and cowboy boots were never meant as protection from the cold. She would wear herself out trying to climb through the snow, and she would freeze to death on the mountainside.

But the alternative was simply to wait while Travis died, and she would feel like a murderer.

After a while the wreckage and the bedrock were hidden from view. She did not know how long or how far she had climbed. She took out one of the plastic strips, warmed it in her hand to make it pliable, and tied it to the branch of a tree.

Immediately she realized how futile it was. She would never even find the tree to see the strip. She should have had a hundred or so to mark an adequate trail, but there had not been time or enough plastic. She would have to count on finding her tracks in the snow.

She was crazy. Crazy. It became a chant that she sang to herself as she trudged on, her breath coming hard, up the hill. She did not even know where she was headed. And when she reached the top, she would see nothing but snow. Just nothing. She was crazy.

It was not hard to imagine herself lost. Travis was right. She should have stayed with the plane. It would take only one gust of wind to erase her footprints, and then she would be gone.

Really and forever gone. No one even knew she had been on that flight. She had told her office only that she was going to Holland Mills. They would assume a commercial flight. She would simply, as far as anyone knew, drop off the face of the earth.

She struggled on through the snow, slipping frequently on the treacherous rock beneath it. The cowboy boots were made for fashion, not for hiking over rough terrain. Finally, exhausted, she flung her arm around a tree and rested. She unzipped her jacket. The upper part of her body was over-heated, but her legs and feet ached with cold.

This was crazy. She ought to have been with Travis, keeping him warm. And watching him die. And not being able to do anything about it.

She raised her head to see where she was, to take her next step. She stared for a moment before she realized that, through the trees, she was seeing a rocky ledge. An outcropping. It seemed to hang in space. A sort of eagle eyrie, she thought. Not the summit of the mountain—she had no idea where that was—but high. If she could reach it without falling on rocks or through snow-covered air, she would have a much higher vantage point than she had had back at the crash site. Maybe worth nothing, but she was too close not to try. If she couldn't see the fire tower from there, she would go back down. The summit itself was too elusive.

The ground grew steeper as she approached the ledge. She slipped and grabbed a small tree to break the fall. She clung to it, unable to pull herself upright. Her head was swimming, her body too weak and uncontrollable. The dizziness was probably not from altitude, but from hunger.

She would never make it. She could not climb that last distance. She looked down the mountain and did not know how she had come as far as she had. It seemed an endless distance. She would never be able to go back. She hadn't the strength.

Then she thought of Travis. Depending on her. If not for her, none of this would have happened. She was responsible for his life.

And Shelley's.

Kevin's sister. Kevin had a sister and no one knew it.

Diane had known it. She had known about Shelley all

along, but she hadn't thought of Kevin as Travis's child. Only her own.

She kept her mind busy so she would not spin or black out or realize that she couldn't make the climb. She pulled herself several more feet up the mountain. But she was no closer to the ledge. She had several yards still to cover. It was impossible. Hopeless. But she couldn't stop now. Probably she really had lost her mind. Grasping at anything. And if she ever reached the ledge and couldn't see the fire tower, she would die. Because there was nothing else.

Again she slipped and fell. It was useless trying to walk upright. The way was too steep and she was too tired. She crawled on her hands and knees, bracing herself against the snow.

She sang softly. Folk songs, college songs. She chanted and recited poetry. Anything to keep from noticing the passage of time. She did not want to think about how long she had been crawling. The ledge was coming closer.

And then what? Suppose she didn't see anything? She would go back down to the igloo and find him dead. And maybe he would have lived if she had not left him.

She was nearly at the ledge. She could try to pull herself up onto it, but she hadn't the strength. She would fall all the way down the mountain.

Climb a little higher, a little way above it. Then she could lower herself onto it. If she didn't slip. What made her think she could see the fire tower, anyway? It was probably all the way around on the other side.

Only a few more feet. Up above the ledge. She turned and looked down. The earth seemed to drop away below her. She closed her eyes.

It was no time for vertigo. She inched her way down onto

the ledge. She tested the rock. And imagined it pulling loose and hurling her into space.

She would not go far out onto it. She remained on her knees, fear gripping her throat, as she surveyed the scene below her.

She could not see the bedrock field. It might have been hidden by trees. Or over to one side. She had no idea whether she had climbed straight up.

But there was the lake. She could see more of it now. She scanned the hills around it for the fire tower.

Nothing. If it was anywhere, it was probably too far away to see.

Just nothing. An empty universe.

She looked again. Her last hope. She had seen villages on the map. Not many. And roads. Maybe they were all buried in snow. Or over the far horizon. She could see nothing, human or animal. Only—

Near the lake. She couldn't be sure. It looked like smoke.

She needed binoculars. She narrowed her eyes. Curled her hands and looked through them.

It couldn't be. Smoke. Rising from the snow. A snow-covered roof? She couldn't see, in all the snow. But it *was* smoke.

"Travis!" she called into the stillness.

She scrambled from the ledge and began to slip and tumble down the mountainside. She bruised her back on a hidden rock and picked herself up again. The way down was almost as hard as it had been coming up, but she followed her own trail in which the snow was partially packed.

From time to time she called out "Travis!" so he would hear her and live. He *was* still alive. He had to be.

Soon she could see the snow-covered plane. She had not climbed as far as she thought. She stopped to clear the snow from its roof and wings. Maybe the shape, if not the color, would make it visible.

She ran, panting, to the igloo. From its entrance she watched until he drew a breath.

She knelt beside him, removed her glove, and touched his face. Her hand was icy.

"Travis, I climbed up the mountain and I saw smoke! Down near the lake, there's smoke! It wouldn't be a forest fire in all this snow. It must be somebody in a cabin, a hunter or an ice fisherman, and they'd have transportation. A snowmobile or something."

She did not want to think that it might be a fisherman or a camper who was as snowbound as she was.

"I'm going down there. I'm going to get help. I'll bring help, Travis. There's somebody there, so be patient. Are you warm enough?"

He was burning up, but he needed outside heat. She put another two sticks on the small fire and watched them catch. When she was sure they would not flare up, she left him again and started down the mountain.

23

Jerry Mercer studied the face in the mug book. He wished he could have seen a profile of the alleged brother, but it wouldn't help to ask her for more pictures. She was hardly what you'd call cooperative.

Still, this was pretty damn close. The subject, in his mug shot, was not as relaxed as in the snapshot, but he didn't look like a relaxed person anyway. It was hard to imagine what the girl saw in him. The face itself wasn't bad-looking, but the expression was cold and stiff, even for a mug shot. And an expression was part of a face.

He borrowed a telephone and called Chuck Baroni.

"I think I've got something here. This Arlie Dean, the guy the Puerto Rican kid identified. There's reason to believe he has some connection with the Wallek girl." He did not want to say any more about last night's expedition. "Can we check him out?"

"Look, Jerry," Baroni said with strained kindliness, "will you let us handle it?"

"Trail's getting cold," Jerry reminded him. "Look, the guy's on parole. If he's our man, he's probably flown the coop. It would be simple to check that with his parole officer. That'd be a sort of confirmation that he might be the one."

"Still doesn't help you find him."

Jerry gnashed his teeth. Baroni added, "Call me back in half an hour."

It was the longest half hour on record. Jerry went out for coffee, but couldn't drink it. He waited twenty-seven minutes, then made the call.

Baroni came on with a purr. "You want to know something? Arlie Dean jumped parole three months ago. He left the rooming house in Manhattan where he was staying, and nobody's seen him."

"Three months ago, huh?"

"Yup. Looks like your identification's pretty flimsy there, Jerry. Why don't you go on what the girl said?"

"Because I think she was lying."

"What makes you think that?"

"I think she was covering up for somebody, and I think it was Arlie Dean. Now look, as a taxpayer and a parent of the victim, I want to know what you guys have got."

"We're working on it."

"You're working on Ty Hannon, right?"

"Among other things. Hannon was the only positive, remember? We'll keep you posted."

Christ, the only positive. "She has you right where she wants you, Chuck."

"Huh? Who does?"

"Wallek."

"Aw, come on."

The conversation was going nowhere. Jerry ended it, but not before he had aged a few more years.

It looked as if he would have to go on alone. It didn't matter that he wasn't officially on this, he was still a cop. He'd take a leave of absence. He'd get a note from his doctor saying he was emotionally disturbed with grief and needed a rest. And he'd go after Arlie Dean by himself. He didn't think Gina was about to tell them he'd been to see her. She had too much to hide.

He checked Dean's credentials one more time. Couldn't seem to hold a steady job. Worked occasionally for brief periods. Seemed to have more money than job record would indicate. It went along with what Gina said, even if she hadn't meant to tell him the truth. Petty burglaries and holdups. He seemed to like holdups. Probably got a macho kick out of guns. Served time in Dannemora. Escaped, recaptured after eighteen months. At time of capture, he was working as a maintenance man in a resort hotel.

Interesting. He came from upstate, too. But would he go back there? More likely he'd head for Mexico or Brazil, if he could get there. Legally or illegally, it took money. The holdup at Jack's hadn't netted him anything. He'd shot Becky before he could collect.

Why the holdup at Jack's? It was not a big money place, but it was all cash, not credit cards or checks. And the cash registers would be full after a whole day. Still, it was likely an impulsive act. That would indicate a drug habit, but his bio didn't say anything about drugs. He just needed money, so he robbed the store where his girlfriend worked, knowing she wouldn't snitch. A dangerous, paranoid person. A young girl moves, and he blows her to pieces without even thinking. A psychopath.

The two cops, too. He was jumpy and paranoid, running from one homicide, so he saw two cops and figured they were after him. Popped them off, again without stopping to think. Undoubtedly, they hadn't been after him, or they would have been more careful.

Crazy but smart. He had figured out how to get away. Where to hide. He didn't seem to be with Gina, although that was his usual address.

179

It was going to be a long haul. The first thing was to find out more about this clown. Where would he be likely to go? Where *had* he been going, ending up in Manhattan like that? Two Hundred Seventh Street. What was there? Two Hundred Seventh and Broadway.

Two people who had been on the scene right after the shooting said the man seemed to be on foot. They hadn't seen where he went. He disappeared around a corner. He could have had a car there, but if he had been in a car, why would he have gotten out to shoot the cops?

Jerry could hear Baroni laughing at him. What made him think it was the same person? He didn't know what made him think it. He only knew that something did. A pair of glasses and a hunch, okay, Chuck?

He drove westward along Fordham Road, picturing a man walking past the stores, the garages, down the steep, winding hill and over the bridge that crossed, first, the Major Deegan Expressway and then the Harlem River.

Now he was in Manhattan. On the street to his left was a warehouse where you could buy discount beer. He had often gone there himself in happier days. Then the Pathmark Supermarket. Open twenty-four hours. Had people been shopping even then, at midnight last Tuesday?

Block after block. He should have done it at night to see what it was like, how many people were around. What was it like for this guy who would walk so far? Where the hell had he been *going?*

When Jerry reached Broadway, he parked his car by a fire hydrant and got out. The thing that immediately struck him was that 207th Street was a continuation of Fordham Road.

The second thing he noticed was the subway station. He started toward it, but on his way he looked around at the

180

buildings. The guy could have a friend here. He could be holed up somewhere. He could be watching right now. Probably spot the old cop even out of uniform.

It was an A train stop.

He had a subway map in the glove compartment, for reference. The A train went all the way down Manhattan and across Brooklyn to Queens.

His brain began to rebel. He couldn't take this. He couldn't do it all by thinking. He wanted lunch, but it was too early for lunch.

What he really needed was to get that Wallek woman to talk. But before that, he would get all the information he could from the Thirty-fourth Precinct. And then maybe it would be lunchtime.

The Thirty-fourth Precinct didn't have much about the man. He had only been seen running away. Nobody had seen him fire the gun. But he had had something in his hand that might have been a gun. And something over his shoulder, like a bag with a strap. And a raincoat, not a jacket.

A large bag. He hadn't had that when he went into Jack's. Unless he left it outside, but you don't leave anything outside in New York City. It wouldn't be there when you came back.

Baroni would say all those differences only proved it was not the same person. But to Jerry it indicated something else. The man had gone home after the holdup, taken a different coat, and grabbed a bag. For what? Because he was going somewhere. He knew Gina would be detained at the store while the police questioned everybody.

From the presence of the bag, it looked as if he meant to take a few days off. He might even have had a contingency plan.

All a wild guess, but it was more than a guess. The timing was right, the body build and the glasses checked out. And there was that unshakable hunch.

He stopped at a newsstand to buy a paper. He always checked the dailies, every one of them, for anything about Becky's death.

He sat in his car and turned the pages. He didn't care about the world news. The world could keep right on going to hell, as far as he was concerned. He couldn't stop it. His job was Arlie Dean. Maybe if Arlie Dean were cleaned off the streets, the world would be that much better.

He didn't find anything about Becky. Only the two cops. No leads so far. Still trying to identify the man seen by witnesses. Jerry couldn't help them there. His identification was all in his mind.

THREE CHILDREN DIE IN UPSTATE FIRE. He shuddered. Three children. He wasn't the only one.

PLANE CARRYING FOUR BELIEVED DOWN IN ADIRONDACKS. Four rich people who could afford a private plane. But it was poignant. Just the day before Thanksgiving.

He tossed the newspaper into a trash basket and started his car. He drove back to the Bronx, back up the hill on Fordham Road, and then down along the street where Gina Wallek lived.

He parked his car, walked to the corner where there was a pay phone, and dialed her number. He could watch the entrance to her building while he talked.

"Miss Wallek? Gina? This is Jerry Mercer, Becky's dad. I hope I didn't wake you."

"Well, you did," was the strained answer, heavy with sleep. He thought he was already reaching her. The first "hello" had been angry, but when she learned who it was, her voice dropped.

"Sorry. I didn't know your hours. But I'm right around the corner and I have a couple more questions. I'll give you a minute to comb your hair, okay?"

There was a pause, and then a reluctant "Okay." She added, "Mr. Mercer, I'm not hiding anything, honest."

"Right. I just want to talk to you."

He gave her as long as it took him to reach the entrance to her building. She buzzed him right in and was standing in the doorway when he arrived at her floor. She wore a blue-fleece housecoat. Her face was puffy and unmade up, her hair in pink plastic rollers.

"What can I do for you, *Jerry?*" She emphasized the name disparagingly. "Do you mind if I make some coffee for myself? Do you want some coffee?"

"That'd be fine, Gina." He stood respectfully at the kitchen table until she asked him to sit down.

Pulling out a chair, he inquired, "Is Arlie here?"

She jumped visibly, nearly dropping the coffeepot. She stared at the running water, and he could almost see her thoughts. Trying to remember whether she had ever mentioned the name to Becky.

Jerry said, "On second thought, I guess he isn't. You left the door to the other room open. It's a one-room apartment, isn't it?"

She gulped and nodded and continued filling the pot.

"You didn't know he was going to come into the store that night, did you?" Jerry went on. "He took you by surprise. You knew he was a punk, but you never thought he'd hold up the place where you work. But you're a real good actress, Gina. You didn't give him away. And then Becky got it. That was tough for you, wasn't it? The cops said you seemed pretty upset when they got there. But not too upset to give a detailed description, right down to the elbow patches on his brown corduroy jacket."

"That's—what the man had on." Gina's voice was faint. "I just told them what I saw."

"Usually when people are upset, they don't notice things like that. And it turns out your description doesn't match the others anyway. You're a fast thinker, I've got to hand it to you. And I guess any girl worth her salt would cover for her boyfriend, especially if he's got a gun and doesn't mind using it on women and kids."

Her arm jerked as she set the coffeepot on the counter. She turned to him, standing stiffly.

"Mr. Mercer, I don't know where he is, honest. He's not here, I swear. I think he came back after— He knew I'd have to wait for the police. I found stuff thrown around. He must have packed some things. He had this goose-down— he had things for cold weather. A goose-down sleeping bag and a coat and vest."

"Cold weather?" Jerry asked and then regretted his visible interest. "Why, doesn't the landlord give you enough heat?"

"It was sort of like a kit. A survival kit, he called it. In case there was a nuclear attack."

"That's what he told you?"

"Yeah." Sheepishly. She added, "I knew he did time. I knew he was an ex-con, but I thought— He said he was doing odd jobs."

"Yeah, he was. With his Saturday night special."

"I guess I wanted to believe him."

"Okay, so you believed him. Where was he planning to go for this nuclear attack? Did he say?"

"No, he never did. Someplace out of the city, I guess."

"Does he have a car?"

"No. I don't think he even drives a car. I don't know, maybe. But I don't think he has a license."

"That wouldn't stop him from driving." But no cars had been reported stolen in that area at that time.

He could have stolen one at gunpoint. Killed the owner.

"Does he have a tan raincoat?"

"I think so. Yes."

"Is it here?"

She went to the other room to check. She came back to report that she couldn't find it.

"Okay, now let's say this nuclear attack is taking place. How was he planning to get out of the city?"

"He didn't tell me. There's a lot of things he didn't tell me."

I'll bet. "Probably means he wasn't going to take you with him. Didn't you ever wonder about that?"

"I guess I didn't worry too much, because I didn't think there was going to be a nuclear attack."

"And you didn't know what he really meant. Okay, so he took his survival kit and headed out of town. He's wanted for homicide, sweetheart. Not only my daughter, but two cops, too. A double cop killing. He'd try to stay as invisible as possible. That leaves out hitchhiking and waiting around bus or train stations."

"Or the airport," she suggested.

"Or the airport. Now, assuming he's the guy who killed the two cops over on Broadway, and I think he is, he might have been heading for the A train. Does he have any friends in lower Manhattan, Brooklyn, or Queens who might own a car, Gina?"

"I don't know. He didn't seem to know too many people. He didn't go around with other people. He didn't even get phone calls."

"A lone wolf. So where'd he take the A train to? Any ideas?"

She had none. Jerry took the subway map out of his pocket and spread it on the table.

"Dyckman Street," he said. "Does that say anything?"

"No." Unhappily. "I never heard of it."

"It's in Manhattan. Upper Manhattan." He ran his finger down the A train route, calling out the stops. None of them meant anything to her.

"Washington Bridge."

"Huh?"

"George Washington Bridge. That's a bus terminal."

"You said he wouldn't go to a bus terminal."

He couldn't deny that he had said it. But those were almost like local buses. If you timed it right, you wouldn't have to wait around.

Still, it had been close to midnight. Maybe the buses didn't run that late.

But wait a minute. It wasn't only a bus station, it was the bridge. You could walk across the bridge.

That's crazy, he thought. Who'd walk to New Jersey?

Plenty of people would. On any nice day and some rotten ones, people poured across the bridge, walking, jogging, bicycling. Maybe even rollerskating. He didn't know about the middle of the night, but he didn't suppose that would stop Arlie Dean.

"Okay," he said, "maybe he took the A train somewhere, or maybe he took it to a Hundred Eighty-first Street and walked across the bridge or took the bus. So he could have gone to Jersey. Any ideas about that?"

The electric coffeepot finished percolating and gave its last few gasps. She jumped up from the table, apparently eager for distraction.

Jerry asked again, "Where would he go in New Jersey?"

"I don't *know*," she wailed. "I told you, I didn't see him. I don't know what to tell you." She handed him his coffee, put a carton of milk and a bowl of sugar on the table, and sat down, her face sullen.

"It's not that I think you're holding out on me," Jerry said as he stirred his coffee. "But sometimes a person might know something she doesn't think is important, and it is. I asked you about friends in Brooklyn or Queens. How about Jersey?"

"I just told you, I don't know of any friends he had."

"Did he ever talk about other places? Brooklyn? Jersey? Ever visit there?"

She sighed, impatient with his obtuseness.

"Well, okay." He sat back as though the business part were over. "You've got a nice place here. You fixed it up real nice. Was it yours before you met him?"

"Yeah, it was. But the rent's high. You wouldn't believe, for this little place."

"I'd believe. Rents are high all over. But it helps if you share it, right?"

She leaned over to rub her ankle. "It helps when he has work," she said. "He doesn't always have work."

Jerry wondered how she had done it. He knew the money at Jack's Fried Chicken was scarcely more than a pittance, and yet she maintained this apartment and sometimes supported Dean. The rest of the money must have come from Dean. It was either feast or famine in the armed robbery business.

But he guessed that Gina was more emotionally than financially dependent. It happened with a lot of women. They'd put up with anything just to have a man around.

He asked, "Does Arlie treat you okay?"

She looked up, surprised. "Yeah. Mostly. Why?"

"Just wondered. Some guys like that can go off their heads sometimes, especially when they've been drinking."

She shrugged, brushing off the notion that it pertained to her. "Some guys like what?"

"Unstable types."

She opened her mouth to speak, then decided against it. There was no argument in favor of Arlie Dean's stability, and she knew it. He had even botched a holdup, his chosen profession, by nervously shooting a sixteen-year-old girl.

She looked miserable, conceding that her lover was explosive, a killer. She had known it for several days, in fact, even if she had blinded herself to it before. Did she still love him? Jerry wondered. Or did she confuse emotional dependence with love?

"Well, I don't know," she sighed.

Jerry did not know what she referred to, but decided to keep on his present tack. "He's good to you?"

"Well, not good, exactly, but he—"

"But he's your guy. You wouldn't want to see him caught."

"I don't know. I—"

"Would you rather see him gunned down sometime? Trying to shoot it out all alone with ten cops and never have a chance? That's what usually happens with a guy like that. At least in prison he's alive."

He drank his coffee and waited to see if his words had any effect.

She rubbed her ankle again. Then she put her hand back on the table and stared at her silver fingernails.

"Is there— I mean, are there any little airports in New Jersey? The kind where they fly private planes from?"

"Sure. They're all over. Why?" He tried to stifle the prickle that started at the back of his neck.

"Because I just thought of something. Do you know what he said once? There was this thing on TV about somebody hijacking a plane to Cuba. He wondered how they got away with it, because airports have so much security. He said he thought it might be kind of easy to hijack a private plane, you know? If you could get on one. Because you don't have to go through security. Nobody'd know if you had a gun. I just thought of that. I don't know if it helps."

He tried to keep his cup from rattling as he set it down.

"It might," he said, glancing at his watch. Jesus, he'd have to get Baroni. "I've gotta be going. Another appointment. Thanks a lot, Gina, for your time and the coffee. I'll be in touch."

She dragged herself to her feet. "Any time, Mr. Mercer."

"I thought it was Jerry."

She seemed to move in slow motion, following him to the door. Suddenly everything was too slow. All he could think of was the phone and Baroni.

She chose that moment to get sentimental. "I don't know if I helped, Jerry. I really loved your kid. I don't know, I'm so mixed up."

He put a big, awkward hand on her shoulder. "You did the right thing, Gina. I'll be seeing you."

He started down the stairs. As soon as he heard her close the door, he began to run. He ran all the way out of the building and down the sidewalk.

He fished in his pocket for a dime, came up with two nickels. He dialed Baroni's special number.

Baroni was out. He would be back sometime that afternoon.

24

The man had something in his hand. Something he was studying, shuffling, appraising one by one. Although they had reached an understanding of sorts, Shelley was still afraid of his secrets. She crept closer for a better look.

"Where did you get those? That's my father's credit cards! Where did you get them?"

She hadn't meant to ask. She knew perfectly well where he must have gotten them.

Calmly he stuffed the cards into his pocket.

"Your father don't need them where he is. And I can use 'em."

"How? What are you going to do?"

"None of your business."

"If you're going somewhere . . ." She began to tremble, her hands, her voice, everything, "are you taking me?"

"For what?"

"You can't leave me here!"

"I can leave you here, because if I take you with me, you'll get in the way."

"No, I won't, I promise! If you'll just get me out of here and tell somebody—a sheriff, or something—"

"I'm not talking to no sheriff."

"But you're a— You said you're a cop."

"I told you my situation. I'm not talking to no sheriff."

"You don't have to talk. Just help me find somebody. A park ranger."

"Help yourself."

"I—I—"

"I don't know," he said. "You don't seem to remember too good about the crash. I don't want you lousing me up."

"I'll remember. I'll tell them anything you want."

He watched her, his eyes cold and frightening. He didn't trust her. She might say the wrong thing. He didn't trust her. Didn't trust her . . .

Hell, Jerry thought, the missing plane.

He went back to his car for the newspaper, then remembered he had thrown it away.

There could have been a lot of other reasons why the plane went down, in a storm like that.

But that was Wednesday. He thought back to Wednesday. The storm hadn't started yet. It was a sunny day.

But windy. That might have done it.

He needed the paper. He thought it said Teterboro Airport, but he couldn't be sure. If it did . . .

He should have left a message for Baroni. But he couldn't wait around all afternoon. It wasn't even twelve yet. He would just have to—

Buy another newspaper. He cruised around until he found a cigar store. They were sold out.

He drove back to Fordham Road, kept driving until he saw a newsstand. Elation! They had the paper. He grabbed one, forgetting his change. He turned to the page, hoping it was the right edition.

Wrong page. He turned them quickly.

PLANE CARRYING FOUR BELIEVED DOWN IN ADIRON-DACKS. He skimmed through it.

191

Teterboro Airport it was.

He was off on a tangent. Nobody'd do a thing like that. Talk about it, maybe, but do it?

Maybe Arlie knew the people on the plane. Who could tell?

A punk like Arlie Dean? Still, it might be worth checking the thing. It would only take a phone call.

It took several phone calls. He got the number from Information and dialed the airport. The person who answered switched him to somebody else. And then a third person.

Finally he learned the plane had been a Cessna Skylane, which meant nothing to him.

"It took off Wednesday about nine forty-five A.M.," they told him, "for Massena, New York. The last radio contact was Schenectady. They've had to delay the search because of heavy snowstorms."

He supposed it might have been heavy upstate. In the city it had been mostly wet snow with no deep accumulation.

"Any way of finding out who was on board?" he asked.

"The names of the passengers? I'm sorry, we don't have that information. Only the pilot's name. You might try checking with Adams Aviation. The plane was one of their rentals."

"You don't have their number—"

The call was over. He was out of change, anyway. He debated getting more change. Or going home to call from there.

Or driving out to Teterboro. It wasn't too far, but the whole thing was a long shot, although maybe not too long. If he got his geography straightened out, he could tell better.

He went back to his car and found a New York State map in the glove compartment. He knew where Dannemora was. He had a vague idea that Schenectady was somewhere up around there. He had never heard of Massena.

Schenectady turned out to be farther south than he had thought. Not far from Albany. And Massena was right up near Canada. And somewhere around there, between Dannemora and Massena, but south of them, Dean had been found at his resort hotel and recaptured.

He turned his car onto Fordham Road and again drove past the shops, the university, down the hill. Across the bridge into Manhattan.

At Broadway he turned south. He would trace the man's route. Find out how likely the whole thing was. Follow the A train. But when he reached Dyckman Street he turned onto the West Side Highway. He had no more patience with stoplights and delays.

At the bridge he began to clock his mileage. He already knew you could walk across it, but he clocked it anyway. Three-quarters of a mile. He followed the signs to Route 46.

It occurred to him that everything had fallen too neatly into place. There had to be a catch somewhere. Probably the guy was in Brooklyn. He had no idea how to find him in Brooklyn, so he kept on driving toward Teterboro Airport.

Six miles. Not too bad a walk. You could do it in a couple of hours.

Except he probably hadn't done it. He probably hitched a ride, if he came this way at all. Maybe even hijacked a car. If you hijacked a car, nobody'd know it. Cars didn't have to file flight plans. Only trouble was, you couldn't get as far as you could in a plane without having contact with other people. Still, it could be done and often was.

Adams Aviation. He nearly missed it. An inconspicuous white trailer. He parked his car, went inside, and identified himself to the man behind the desk.

"Police?" said the bewildered man. "New York City police?"

"It's about that missing plane," Jerry said.

"The Skylane?" Bill Adams looked still less enlightened. "I rented that to a guy I've known for years. He's a good pilot. Had good flying weather. I don't understand it. But what's it got to do with the police?"

"Who else was on the plane?"

"His daughter and another woman, I remember. And—yeah, wait. There was this guy, this businessman, had to get to Montreal. His wife was very sick."

"Did you know him, too?"

"Never saw him before. He came to my office early, before Andrews got here. That's the pilot. Said he had to get to Montreal, couldn't afford the regular fare, and asked if anybody was going that way."

Another tightening in his chest. He should have brought somebody along. He was going to have a heart attack for sure before this was over.

"Can you describe him?"

"I don't know. Raincoat. I think he wore glasses. Why? What's up, Lieutenant?"

"I'm not—"

"Wait, it's coming back to me. I think he was maybe a little smaller than you. Shorter. Uh—thinner. I'll tell you, I didn't think too much about it. I remember the raincoat. He looked like a businessman."

"Any beard? Mustache?"

"Not that I can remember."

Of course he had shaved it off on that quick trip back to Gina's apartment.

194

Hell, he wished he had a picture. He should have asked her. He doubted that she would have given him one.

"Did he give his name?"

"Not to me."

"Would anybody have his name? Aw, forget it. He'd have used a phony anyway. Do people do that often? I mean, hitching a ride like that on a private plane?"

"Well, no, I can't say they do, but I knew there was a lot of problems with the fog we had just before that. A lot of airports shut down. And then the holiday travel. I figured it was hard getting a seat on a regular flight, even if you could afford it. It made sense to me. And the guy was pretty desperate. Look, Lieutenant, do you mind telling me what's going on?"

"No, I'll tell you," Jerry said, "if you'll stop calling me Lieutenant. I just wanted to check the identification first. I know it's a wild shot, but I have a hunch this guy might have tried to hijack a private plane. His girlfriend told me he described a plan like that once."

He watched Bill's face dissolve into a look of shock and surprise. And then grow red as he shouted, "Dammit to hell, you really think that's what happened?"

"I think it *might* have happened," Jerry answered. "I'm trying to find the man, and that's the only possible lead I have so far. He killed a young girl and two police officers."

"Was it the same guy? I read about that."

"I think. And then he disappeared off the earth. It was just a guess that he might have headed this way, but from what you tell me—"

"Sorry I can't be more definite about the face."

"Understandable." Jerry was lost in thought. "Now, the next step. Did they start a search for the plane yet?"

"Soon as they can. The conditions are still pretty bad up there. The runways are covered, and there's a lot of blowing."

"Any idea where they'll start? And how I can get there?"

"How come— Are you all by yourself? Don't they usually—"

"Yes, I'm on my own. The guys who got the case are barking up other trees, but I know I'm right. And the girl who was killed—she was my daughter."

"Jesus, man, why didn't you tell me?"

"I, uh—"

Bill came around the desk and clapped Jerry on the shoulder. "Look, Lieutenant, I'm in this, too. I got suckered into it, and Andrews—he's a friend of mine. And I've got kids of my own. So here's what we're gonna do. We're going up there in my plane. And we're going now."

"You mean that?"

"I mean it. You ready? Let's go."

25

Diane had never imagined it would be so far down the mountain. Not like this. She went on forever, running, stumbling through deep snow, falling because she could not hold herself up. Twice she blacked out.

After a while she could no longer see the lake. She could only guess at its direction. She had thought that, at this point, she would be nearly there. Instead, the snowy forest stretched into eternity. It had been deceptive, looking down from the ledge. Dips and folds in the earth had been invisible.

It occurred to her that she might be headed in the wrong direction. She didn't want to think about it. There was nothing she could do. No sun to tell her which way she was going. Only low gray clouds. All the forest looked the same. And there was no longer just one downhill, but endless ups and downs.

And then suddenly she was there. She couldn't believe it. She had been seeing the lake and didn't know it. Frozen and covered with snow, it was only a vast white thing through the trees, like everything else.

Almost there. She could no longer feel her own body. She was nothing but a presence moving through the woods. As though she had died.

A few more yards. And then there were no longer trees in the way. She had reached the lake.

197

With the next step, she slipped on a rock. The fall wrenched her ankle, and she sat down in the snow, her eyes watering with pain.

She tried to get up. Oh my God, she thought, I can't stand up.

She had no strength. None at all, even to rise to her feet. She thought maybe Travis was dead by now and it didn't matter.

And then she knew she could never believe that. Not about Travis. He *must* be alive. It was the only thing that would keep her going.

I love him, she thought. I really love him.

She turned over onto her hands and knees and somehow managed to climb to her feet. The smoke. Must find the smoke. She was sure it had come from a cottage. It could not have been a camp fire, not in this cold. But any fire. Anything.

Please be a park ranger with a telephone. Please call a rescue helicopter. He's dying up there.

She looked to the left and the right. She had no idea where the smoke might be. She couldn't see it now. There was nothing but trees.

She would try the left. If necessary, walk all around the lake. Something would have to be there.

She began to fantasize. A cabin with a snowmobile and plenty of fuel. She could follow her tracks up the mountain and bring him down herself.

Ranger headquarters with a telephone. A helicopter parked on the ice and someone to fly it. Blankets and food. A warm fire.

A telephone.

A helicopter.

She stopped abruptly and stared at the cabin. Again she

felt disembodied. The cabin was there and she did not exist.

She looked up at the roof, but saw no smoke. Something inside her began to fold. It could not have been an illusion. The cabin was real. Maybe they had let the fire go out.

Or maybe they had gone away.

She hurried toward it. Something about the little house did not seem alive, but she refused to believe it. She reached the front door. It had been padlocked, but the lock was broken. She opened it.

Empty. No one was there. No rangers. In the center, a little way out from the back wall, was a cold wood stove. Wooden bunk beds with no bedding. Shelves built onto the wall were dirty and nearly bare.

She walked over to the stove and touched it. It really was cold. A few scraps of wood were piled in front of it. If she could somehow bring Travis down, she could make a fire to keep him warm.

But she would never be able to bring him without transportation. A snowmobile. Even a sled.

How could the stove be so cold? The whole interior of the cabin was icy cold. She found an empty can with a label that showed ripe peaches and some frozen liquid at the bottom. A partly used bag of sugar with a hole in it. She could eat some of the sugar for energy. But all around the bag were mouse droppings. She turned away and held her mouth to keep from throwing up.

There couldn't have been anyone here this morning. Couldn't have been a fire in the stove even several hours ago.

If there was one cabin by the lake, there must be others. She would have to go on. And if she couldn't get help, she would have to climb all the way back up the mountain.

Maybe she could make a sledge for Travis out of pine branches. Or pull the space blanket across the snow. But he needed medical help.

She left the cabin, carefully closing the door behind her so the wind would not blow it open. She continued on around the lake.

She walked on the ice because it was smoother. A gentle, frigid wind began to blow. Farther out on the lake, she saw plumes of snow rising in the wind.

It would cover her tracks. She would never find her way back up the mountain.

Now it blew all around her, lifting the snow. A miniature blizzard. She felt the crystals stinging her face. It made her walk with her head down, her eyes nearly closed.

Suddenly, for just an instant, she smelled it. Then it was gone. Wood smoke.

She must have been dreaming. A mirage, because she wanted it.

Then another whiff. It came and went in the wind. She began to run. The snow was blowing thickly now. She could scarcely see where she was going. Barely saw the dark thing in front of her.

My God, a wall. She stumbled toward it and reached out her hand. She felt rough wood.

And the door. She could see the door. If the cabin had not been so close to the lake, she would have missed it altogether. She turned the knob and pushed open the door.

A startled face. A cascade of red-gold hair.

"Shelley! Oh my God, *Shelley!*"

In an instant her eyes took in the blue duffel bag, spilling its contents onto a cot.

"He's here? Is he here?"

It was only Shelley. But those were his things. He would be back.

"Shelley, come quick! I'll help you." She held out her hand.

Shelley pulled back. "No, I have to wait."

"But this is your chance! Where did he go?"

The girl's face twisted. "You don't understand. He's a policeman. He's going to get me out of here."

"A policeman? You're crazy. He's the one who made us crash. Don't you remember?"

Shelley began to cry. "No, that's wrong! He's— No!"

Diane held the door open. In the blowing snow a little distance away, something moved. It was gray in the mist, and it moved toward her.

"Quick! He's coming!"

"*No!*" Shelley howled. "I have to *wait*."

"Oh, hurry! I'll take you to your father. He's alive. He's waiting for you."

The snow blew aside, and Diane saw the man's face. For one instant they stared at each other. And then she ran.

The snow held her like quicksand. She heard an explosion. Felt something brush her cheek.

She ran toward the trees. The snow blew thickly. If she could hide in the snow. A little farther. Just a little farther and she would be hidden.

She couldn't do it. He was gaining on her. She tried to run faster but the snow held her down.

She saw where the slope began. She wanted to go up it, but she couldn't. Too weak. She ran on blindly.

The other cabin. If she could get inside—

But she could never hold the door against him. He would trap her there.

Run on. And on. Until she fell dead. Or he gave up.

She could hear him panting. The crunching of snow.

Her legs slowed. She couldn't move them any more. Then she realized she was running uphill.

She did not know where. Not to Travis. She would not lead him to Travis. She dived through the bushes in any place that looked clear. All the leaves were gone. There was no place to hide.

Fatigue crushed her chest. Her breath came hard, big gulps that froze her throat.

Then the air exploded.

He had fired again. She must get away.

She couldn't move. Her heart was bursting. Her legs were dead, glued to the ground.

The trees opened ahead of her. It was clear. Nothing to hide her. The ground sloped downward. Bare snow.

Another shot. She hurled herself into the snow. She was rolling downhill. Sliding and rolling. Over and over. She saw the sky and white snow. A stone struck her back. She cried in pain. And then she was in the air, falling free.

She landed in a deep drift. She lay gasping, cradled in the snow, as something red grew beside her.

Blood red. She watched it spreading through the snow. Her blood.

He had shot her.

She couldn't get up. Couldn't move at all. She could only lie in the snow, feeling her life ebb away, and think of what she had done. She had left Shelley. Had run to save herself. She could have held him off and given Shelley a chance. She was no good. Never any good. Always failed. Always, always. And Travis . . .

26

They had been flying over the Hudson River for more than an hour. The ground below them was covered with snow.

"By the time we get there, it'll be dark," Jerry said.

"Naw. We'll have a little time."

"Then what? How do we even know where to start?"

"Last radio contact was Schenectady. They'd probably follow the flight plan. But look, with the snow, it's not going to be easy. The plane was mostly white, see. Unless some of 'em are alive to send up a signal." Bill turned to Jerry, who knew criminals as Bill knew planes. "If they were hijacked, do you think the punk would leave anybody alive?"

"Hard to say. Every punk is different. We don't even know his overall plan. First thing, I guess, is to look for the plane. But we don't even know that. He might have diverted it somewhere. Any way you can tell if a private plane was diverted?"

"If it landed at an airport, we'd have heard," Bill replied. "Any place else, I couldn't tell you. That means they didn't refuel, anyway."

"So we don't know what we're looking for, or where."

"That's about it. But we're going to start from Schenectady area."

Start. Good God, Jerry thought. They'd have to cover the whole Adirondacks. And it was still only a guess.

Mike Corder was restless that Friday. He had the day off, and all he could do was pace the floor. Ellen was knitting something while Natti watched television. Twice during the commercial breaks there had been appeals for AB negative blood for a three-year-old patient at Memorial Hospital in Holland Mills.

"I wish they'd stop," Ellen said after the second one. "It doesn't make sense during a children's program. Children can't give blood."

"Ellen—" He didn't know what else to say. He loved that girl, but she lived in a world of her own. A world that began and ended with Ellen. It had taken him years to admit that to himself, and he wished it weren't true.

"Why don't you sit down?" she asked. "You're driving me nuts."

"Anything you say." He sat down and picked up the newspaper. He had already skimmed through it, but there was nothing else to do. He couldn't cope with a book, the way he felt.

He passed up the article on AB negative blood. It depressed him. Marian had said Diane had that blood type. Marian had said Diane was practically on her way up Tuesday night. Here it was Friday. His legs felt jumpy, and he knew he would have to start pacing again. He turned the page.

THREE CHILDREN DIE IN FIRE. He looked over at Ellen. It made him sick to read things like that. It made him remember the time the kitchen was on fire because she hadn't cleaned the broiler, and it made him remember the time she had been gabbing on the phone with Natti in the tub, and Natti had slid under the water. He had come home to find Ellen carrying her and screaming and crying, expecting sympathy because she was so worried about Natti.

SMALL PLANE LOST OVER ADIRONDACKS. Four Aboard. Who, he wondered, would be fool enough to fly in this weather?

The plane had been missing since Wednesday morning. That made a little more sense.

"Hey!" he yelped. "Travis Andrews! Isn't that her name?"

Ellen looked up from her knitting. "Who?"

"Diane. Isn't that his name? Travis Andrews of New York City. Isn't that the man she married?"

"What about him?"

"He was piloting a plane from New York to Massena Wednesday morning. They think it crashed."

"Huh?" She still did not get the connection.

"New York to Massena, right? Wednesday morning. That's exactly when she would have tried to come, and if he's the father—"

"I don't know what you're talking about." Ellen took up her knitting again. "She hasn't seen Travis in years. She said he went to Brazil. And why would she be coming up that way when there are perfectly good regular planes?"

"Maybe she couldn't get a flight. The airports were pretty jammed up."

"How do you know?"

"I called the airline. I wanted to know what flight she might be on."

He had a vague impression of Ellen with her mouth open, looking as though he had just clouted her. He didn't care. Diane—down in the mountains. Jesus Christ. Trying

205

to get to her baby. She might even be dead, but he couldn't handle that.

He heard Ellen's angry voice. "There are probably a million Travis Andrews. Who are you calling?"

"Marshall."

"Who's Marshall?"

"Guy I know who has a friend with a plane."

He didn't hear the rest of what she said. He saw Diane huddled in the fuselage, trying to keep warm. He dialed Marshall's number. Through the ringing, Ellen said, "She probably wasn't on it."

Marshall said he would get back to him. He did, twenty minutes later. By then Mike was putting on his boots and parka.

"Where are you going?" Ellen demanded. "You're not really going out to look for her!"

"Do you want me to sit on my can while your sister freezes to death?"

"But you don't even know where to look. That's a big place out there."

"They were heading toward Massena. The last contact was Schenectady, so they're somewhere between."

"But this is crazy. What if she wasn't on the plane?"

"Whether she was or wasn't, four people were, and they deserve to be found, don't they?"

"But what do you care—"

"I care. Would you want it to be you?"

She snapped. "You're just trying to make me feel guilty."

"Guilty? About what?"

"Because—because it happened. I should have been watching him."

"You should have been, but quite frankly, Ellen, just now I wasn't even thinking about you. I was thinking about the people on that plane. They're out there freezing, and it's got nothing to do with you feeling guilty or not guilty. Try to see beyond yourself, okay, hon?"

He left and she heard his car starting. He hadn't even said good-bye. He hadn't kissed her. And it was all because of Diane.

The first thing Diane felt was the pain in her arm. A burning pain. She opened her eyes and saw that her blood had frozen in the snow.

The snow was everywhere, even against her face. She was buried in it, but she could breathe. She tilted back her head and saw the sky. She was down in a hole of snow, but she could see the sky. Low and gray. It wasn't snowing, but she was down inside the snow. Like a cradle. A womb. Mother earth. She was back where she belonged.

Then she remembered Shelley. She tried to sit up, but she couldn't. Maybe it was the snow. It held her down. Mother earth. It was not her time to be born yet. She snuggled down into it, feeling the creeping numbness in her ears, her hands and legs.

Her mind floated up to the igloo, the warmth of Travis, the comfort of his body, the fire. If she could follow her mind up the side of the mountain, she would be there.

She saw him floating toward her, smiling.

From time to time he woke. He thought he was alone now. He couldn't feel her or hear her voice. Maybe not for a long time. His eyes opened in shock. Dead. She had died.

But where?

And then a calmness spread over him. He was glad, in a way, that she had gone before him. It meant she would not have to be alone.

He couldn't do anything about her. Or about anything.

But he was bothered. It took him a while to realize why. He should be fighting. It was the fighters who survived.

You know what? he said to himself. I don't give a damn.

Still, it seemed rather weak just to let things happen to him. He turned his head.

The fire was out. Only a few charred pieces of wood. It was cold, too, there in the igloo.

Suddenly it seemed very funny that he was there in an igloo, all alone, and the fire was out, and he was too weak to move, and his body was full of burning, stabbing, crushing aches. He began to laugh. How in the hell—

But he wasn't laughing. He realized he wasn't laughing. He was only lying there staring up at the snowy ceiling.

It was *real*, that snowy ceiling. It was reality, and he was here. And somewhere outside, very far away, the sound of engines. And there was no one to light the signal fire.

Or maybe the sound was only in his head.

27

"My father's alive," Shelley told him.

"Who says?"

"That woman."

"She's lyin'."

"How do *you* know?"

"Because I seen him dead, okay?"

"Maybe he wasn't—"

She did not know what to think. The woman had gotten her all mixed up. For a while everything had been all right. The cop was going to help her. Now she wasn't sure he was a cop, and she was afraid of him.

She began to cry. She heard swift steps as he came toward her. Before she could get out of the way, he hit her on the head. A sharp crack with his gun. She went down in a wave of stars. Down and up. The pain devoured her.

My father is alive. Alive, alive, alive.

He shouted something at her. She couldn't hear him through the stars.

He jerked her arm, pulling her upright. The blackness gradually cleared from her head.

"She said he's alive?"

"That's what she said." A tiny bit of hope. "If you could just take me to my father."

She had to be careful. He might hit her again.

He let go of her arm and began to pack his duffel. They were going somewhere. Or at least he was.

"Where are you going?"

He nodded toward the door. She hoped he wouldn't take her. After he left, she would go and find her father.

He sat down on the bed and opened his gun. He was loading it, putting more bullets in it. Her father . . .

"No," she said.

He looked up. "No, what?"

"Don't—use that."

He stared at her. It seemed a long time. Then he asked, "You telling me what to do?"

"No, I—" She had made him angry. "Can I go with you?"

He pocketed the gun. "I'll come back for you."

"Where are you going now?" Her father. He was going to kill her father. He knew how to get there and she didn't.

"I said I'll come back for you."

"*Please* let me go!"

He shouldered the duffel bag and strode out the door. He had no intention of returning, or he would not have taken the duffel.

"*Please,*" she cried, running after him. He did not look back but went on walking. She floundered through the snow, trying to keep up with him.

They were over the Adirondacks now. How many square miles? Jesus.

"Impossible to see anything in this snow," Bill Adams said.

"Maybe there's nothing to see," Jerry answered.

"That's true, too."

"Wait a minute. What's that down there?"

"A lake. It's not quite frozen in the middle."

"No, over there. It looks like a house. And there's smoke!"

"Somebody's keeping cosy."

"Where there's smoke coming out of a chimney," Jerry said, "there's people. Maybe they saw something. Any way we can get down there?"

"Down *there?*"

"Can you land on the lake?"

"I wouldn't trust it. What do you want to get down there for?"

"Like I said, they might have seen or heard a plane in trouble."

"Well, I can't land here. Anyhow, Lieutenant, don't get carried away. There's a lot of territory here. There's even people. This isn't the Antarctic. Let's wait till we have something to go on."

"Okay, okay, you're right. I guess I was sorta carried away." Jerry settled back to watch again for a downed plane. Every time he thought he saw something, it turned out to be snow-covered trees or rocks.

Diane fought her way again to the surface. It was Shelley's gloves on her hands that reminded her.

I can do it.

She had to do it. She had run away and left the girl. It wasn't Shelley's fault the man had lied to her. Even brainwashed her. It happened to plenty of older people, too.

She raised her head. The wind had died down. She could see through the trees and she didn't see him anywhere. He was gone. Back to Shelley. She would have to find the cabin again. But be careful this time.

She did it slowly, packing the snow with her hand and pushing herself up onto it. Step by step. A kind of manual elevator. Every minute or two she had to stop and wait out the pounding, the burning in her arm.

Finally she was up. She was standing. In deep snow. Above her, a cliff about twelve feet high. On its rim she could see a break in the snow where she had run and fallen. And lumps of snow stained with red.

She would have to get up there somehow. Maybe climb up the rocks on one side.

Her arm hurt like the blazes. It knotted her stomach and made her want to throw up. She wished the cold would numb it.

Up the rocks. One at a time. Take it easy. Gain a foothold, then rest.

Her foot slipped. She grabbed a branch, forgetting her arm. She held on tight and retched with the pain.

When it eased a little, she stood for a long time, considering. But this was the only way, back up here. To Travis and Shelley.

Another step up. Another. Her hands and feet were numb. That was why she had slipped. She tried not to look up or down. Tried not to think about getting anywhere. Only about each step as it came, until finally she reached the top.

Then she looked down. I did it, she thought. How did I do it?

She set out along the trail they had made, she and the man. She felt as though she had run for miles trying to get away from him. She hoped it was not as far as she remembered.

After a while she could see the lake. Down a hill, through the trees, through tangled bushes. It was the lake she had set out to find, where she hoped the fire tower was.

She looked up suddenly, hearing a sound. In all that silent snow, a low humming sound.

An engine.

A plane.

She could *see* it. Over the treetops. And then it was gone.

She ran up the next hill, waving her arm, but it was gone.

"Come back!" she screamed, forgetting the man and his gun. Forgetting everything except Travis and that she had gone off and there was no one to light the signal fire.

Slowly she folded into the snow. It was their only chance, and she had blown it.

28

If he could only crawl out of the igloo, Travis thought, they could see him. From time to time he dreamed that he was out. That he was somehow standing. Lighting the signal fire. And then he would realize it was only a dream.

If he could reach his pocket, he could check to see if the matches were there. But he couldn't reach his pocket, and it was only a dream that he needed matches anyway. He was nowhere near the signal fire. He was lying on his back on the ground and it was chilling him through and through.

He remembered her going out several times to clear off the signal fire. He wondered what had happened to her. Had she fallen over the side, going out in the snow?

But that was a long time ago. Time had passed since then, he thought. Waking and sleeping.

Christ, how long have I been here?

Some sense memory told him that, not so long ago, he had felt her body warm against his. Maybe even just a few hours ago she had gone off and left him.

Something about a fire tower. He remembered now. She was going to go for help.

Sonofabitch, it was the worst thing she could have done. And all for him, because he was weakening. If he could have just hung in there—then maybe she could have hung on, too. Sonofabitch.

She couldn't find her own tracks coming down from the mountain. The snow had blown over them. It had covered up her trail. She would never find her way back to him.

Again she had failed, done the wrong thing. Again and again, all her life. And this, perhaps, was the most terrible thing of all, because it was a man's life. A man she loved.

The cabin was ahead of her. A screen of trees hid her from it. She hoped her light-blue jacket would blend with the shadows in the snow.

Somehow she would have to get Shelley. Somehow. But how? He would see her first. The cabin had windows on all sides.

She moved closer, dodging from one bare bush to another. She didn't see any smoke coming from the chimney. Would they have let the fire go out?

And then she saw tracks in the snow. A human trail. It went up a slight incline into the woods from the jumble of tracks all around the house. Maybe he had made the tracks when he came and caught her earlier. She could tell nothing about them, how many people, or which direction they were headed. It was only a trail of disturbed snow.

So it must have been more than one person or more than one direction.

She waited, listening. She did not hear anything. There was no reason why she should. The windows were all closed. Maybe he was waiting for her to come back. But he probably thought he had left her for dead.

She realized that if he were watching from the house, he could see her. The bare trees did not give enough cover.

Not even the thickets of bushes. He could see her and he did nothing. Maybe waiting for her to come closer.

She was wasting time. They could be getting farther and farther away. She forced herself closer to the house. At any moment he would fire. She could almost feel it in her forehead.

She crept around a corner and saw the front door wide open. Gone. They were gone. But still, in case it was a clever trap, she moved carefully. She looked inside. Gone.

When the door was closed behind her, she began to feel some warmth from the stove. She went over and rested her hands on it. She thought she could stay there forever, feeling the warmth. Why had they left it?

But they had. He had taken his blue duffel bag and the things that had been spilling out of it, so evidently he did not intend to come back. She had it to herself. She could build up the fire again. And there was food. Cans of it on the shelves. She could stay and keep warm. Track an SOS on the lake as she had done on the rock—

Her SOS must be gone, blown away in the wind. There was nothing, no way for anyone to know he was there. She would have to find her way back.

Or Shelley. He would want her to take care of Shelley. To get her home, to safety.

She would never find Shelley. They had a long head start on her. She would never find her way back to Travis. If she stayed in the cabin, she would live. There was Kevin. *Live*.

And Shelley, out in the wilderness with a killer. And Travis. He had been alive when she left him. Travis, sick and helpless. Shelley, a child. It was all up to her.

She warmed her hands for another moment and then went out again. Soon the cold reached her as it had before. She looked around, wondering where to go. Try to find her trail down from the mountain? There might be some remnants of it left.

She could not even find her trail at the edge of the lake. Nothing, except the tracks that went up the slope. Where Shelley had gone. If she was not in the cabin, she must have gone this way. Her fingers and feet were beginning to burn. Only a short time in the cabin and they had thawed enough to be sensitive now. She could have stayed.

Again she had to drown her mind in thoughts. But her thoughts all hurt. Kevin. Travis. Think of her job. The Dow Jones average for the day. Which day? She did not know what day it was.

She caught her breath and stood still. There was that sound again. A plane.

She heard it, but didn't see it. She began to run. A blackness came over her and she slowed again to a walk. She was sinking. Should have eaten something at the cabin. It was too late now. She walked as fast as she could without blacking out, following their tracks to more open ground where she might be seen.

It was a long strip, clear of trees. A ribbon of clear snow, winding, dipping, disappearing into the woods. It did not occur to her that it might have been a road.

29

Ann Lightner had lived in the mountains all her life. She knew very well that a storm like the one on Thursday could happen, but this year she had been preoccupied with her husband's recent stroke and in helping him get back on his feet. She had put off her shopping for a couple more days, till maybe the weekend. There'd be plenty of leftovers from the dinner at her daughter-in-law's.

"God help us," she had said to Earl when she looked out of the window on Thanksgiving morning, "we'll never make it to the kids' for dinner, and all we have in the house is a package of frozen fish."

"Fine with me," replied her ever-philosophical husband. And so they had dined on cod fillets, and that was the last of it, except for some odd cans of soup, a few packets of Jell-O, and a bit of cocoa. It seemed likely they would starve to death, but early on Friday afternoon the weather cleared a little. The snow had stopped and the wind died down. She cleared the area in front of the shed, hauled out the snowmobile, and set off for the village of Sam's Bend, six miles away.

She reached the main road—so called because it was public and the biggest road around—and discovered they hadn't plowed it yet. It wasn't main enough for *that*. Good thing she had the snowmobile. She didn't know how you could manage without one, although her parents had, back in their day. You just did a lot more for yourself then, instead of relying on supermarkets.

She swerved frantically as a figure stepped out into her path. God help us, she thought, braking quickly. It was a young woman in a white parka. She looked pale and pinched and absolutely terrified. Ann waited as the girl came toward her. It *was* a girl, she could see now. A very young girl. Her teeth were chattering.

"Can you help me?" the girl whimpered. "I was in a plane crash and I'm hurt."

"You poor thing." Ann moved forward so the girl could get on the mobile in back of her.

"Uh—there's somebody with me." The voice was high and frightened.

Almost before Ann could absorb the words, a man stepped out of the bushes at the side of the road. Ann registered only a fleeting impression of sunglasses, stubble, and a tan parka as he elbowed the girl aside.

"Get movin'," he said to Ann.

She blinked at him. Dimly she realized he didn't mean the mobile, he meant *her*. And he had a gun. Dazed, she climbed off the snowmobile, and she thought of Earl and that she would have to walk all the way home without any groceries.

Then the gun pointed toward her, and she began to run. The first shot winged the hood of her parka. The second struck her shoulder, and she pitched forward into the snow, where she lay in a sea of pain and cold.

Shelley flew onto the back of the snowmobile. "You're not going to kill my father!"

But he was wheeling in an arc, and she crouched, clinging tightly. Her mind went gray. She didn't understand.

219

Anything. He had shot that woman, that nice-faced, grand-motherly woman. She didn't think it in words, but only felt it. She didn't think of what would come next. Not the moving blur that loomed suddenly in front of them.

Diane had almost reached them. She could even see them, but they couldn't see her, because they didn't know she was there. The bushes hid her. She saw them stop, saw his hand reach out and hold Shelley back, and heard a whine in the distance.

Too high-pitched for an airplane. She had been in the city too long. A snowmobile.

He ducked back into the bushes. He could have seen her, but he was watching the road. He sent Shelley on ahead. Shelley, as white as her jacket. She thought he would leave Shelley and take the mobile, but then she saw the rider get up.

She started to run. The idling snowmobile drowned the sound of her crashing through the bushes. He didn't know to listen. Didn't know she was there. It was her only chance to get Shelley. That was all she thought of. Get Shelley. Get Shelley.

Then Shelley jumped onto the mobile. Screaming about her father.

A heavy branch, almost a log, blocked the way. Diane seized it. He was turning the mobile. Never dreamed she was there. Her only chance.

She rushed out to meet him.

Her ally was surprise. He never expected. His face flashed amazement as she swung the branch at his head.

"Quick, Shelley!"

The snowmobile overturned. He rolled to his knees, reached for the gun. The branch had flown out of her hand when she struck. She lunged for it and swung again. And again. And again, for Travis. For Shelley. For herself and Kevin, while Shelley moaned like an injured animal.

I killed him, she thought and looked up at the throbbing in the sky.

30

"I killed him," she said to the men who came out of the helicopter.

"You darn near did," the gray-haired one told her. "I won't even have to put cuffs on him."

"Will you take me to Holland Mills? I have to get there. My little boy—"

"We'll get you there, don't worry." The man had to support her as she walked. She heard him add something about "Lucky thing we got the copter. Couldn't land a plane here."

She raised her head. Travis hadn't been able to land there, either.

"Travis," she said and pointed. Arnold Dearborn had known the way. "Up there."

Much later, Mike found her in the Holland Mills hospital. She was crying. He put his arms around her to comfort her.

"It's okay, Diane, really. Kevin'll be okay now."

"I know. But he's so—he's so *hurt*. And Travis," she sobbed.

"Isn't Travis all right, too?"

"They took him to Schenectady. I wanted him here with Kevin and me."

"He couldn't have made the trip, Di."

"I know." She finally looked at him and saw that it was Mike. She had forgotten Mike existed. "What are you doing here?"

"I was out looking for you. We heard on the radio that they found you."

"Looking for me?"

"Yes, it was in the paper. Your husband—"

They both turned and saw Ellen standing in the doorway. She looked very small and very sad.

Diane said, "He's not my husband. He never was. He's just the only man I care about."

"Then how come—"

"It's a long story, Mike."

Ellen stared down at the floor. "I guess there are a lot of long stories," she said huskily.

Neither knew what she meant, and they quickly forgot about it as the telephone rang beside Diane's bed. She reached for it with her good arm. Ellen moved, too late, to hand it to her.

"Diane? Miss Hastings? This is Shelley. My dad wants to talk to you, but he can't."

"Oh . . ." said Diane.

"He wants to know how your little boy is."

"Tell him he's okay. He'll be all right now. They didn't want me to give blood, but I did." She heard the words relayed at the other end and asked, "How's your dad?"

"He has pneumonia," Shelley said. "He never had pneumonia before. And he wants me to tell you you're remarkable."

"I'm what?"

"What you did. Everything you did. He says you're a powerful lady."

Was that good or bad? Diane wondered.

"He says," Shelley went on, "he says he's afraid to ask you because you might say no, but—this is very embarrassing."

"Is he there?" asked Diane. "Can he talk at all?"

"Just a minute."

There was a pause, and then she heard Travis's voice, weak and breathy.

"Hi. I shouldn't make her do it. She's embarrassed."

"Do what, Travis?" The sound of his voice . . .

"Ask you—tell you I don't want to lose you. Ask if we can get married as soon as we're out of here."

"Sooner," she said, without thinking. "Get yourself transferred. And bring Shelley. You might as well start explaining to her."

"I read you," he said. "We'll be up on the next plane."